The Lies and Tells of Compost Mckenzie

The Lies and Tells of Compost Mckenzie

Natalie Hynde

© Natalie Hynde 2024. All rights reserved.
No part of this book may be reproduced or transmitted by any means without written permission from the author.

Disclaimer

This is a work of fiction.

Characters, events and dialogue within the narrative are entirely fictional and any resemblance to actual persons, living or dead, or to real events, is purely coincidental and unintended. Readers are advised to consult a qualified healthcare professional for accurate information regarding any mental or other health-related issues and the responsible use of medications.

Troubador Publishing Ltd
Unit E2 Airfield Business Park,
Harrison Road, Market Harborough,
Leicestershire. LE16 7UL
Tel: 0116 2792299
Email: books@troubador.co.uk
Web: www.troubador.co.uk

ISBN 978 1805145 172

British Library Cataloguing in Publication Data.
A catalogue record for this book is available from the British Library.

Printed and bound in Great Britain by 4edge Limited
Typeset in 10.5pt Adobe Garamond Pro by Troubador Publishing Ltd, Leicester, UK

Hotel

It had taken me eighteen months to accept her disappearance.

The agent I was tasked to work alongside when attached to a surveillance team in North Kensington.

Bex was an anarchist with a love of pizza, crisps and fish. Alcoholic drug addict with severe mental health problems and a genius in her own right.

The washing machine is on, and it crosses my mind that it's been weeks since I last put a load on.

I begin to meditate on the subtlety of the mess, the ruin that has disorganised itself in a corner beneath the kitchen window, next to a waste-paper basket and a few white shirts still in the packet. Underneath are receipts and scrunched-up bits of used cotton wool. Above the corner of stacked mess, a packet of pears, two of them missing. I'd eaten one and the other had got lost. A pot of heather and a money plant, some little ornaments on top of the microwave. A couple of nail varnishes, a tiny figure of a Hindu god, a bit of dried coral, a rose quartz, and an Apache tear.

Her eyes, blue like cracked porcelain, had merged with the slate-grey sky out near the docks at King's Cross. Underneath the imitation cockney there'd been an elegance that had hinted towards a good education, but she wasn't posh. Parrots in her eyes. Hair the colour of corn. Bex always wore an old RAF coat and an original Lock & Co bowler – stolen from the Cordings on Piccadilly. The wind had been throwing the trees about as I'd tried to make out her exact words, but I'd been too drunk. Now she's lost and gone forever. I'm pen pals with a ghost. It doesn't ever occur to me that I've killed her, not on this timeline.

It takes all the energy I have to switch on the kettle. I try to open a soup that has unusually been presented in a jar instead of a can but can barely find the strength to do so. After struggling with the lid for several minutes, I realise I have moisturiser on my hands.

Increasingly, I feel my energy draining away. There must be a progression, there must be a change.

I move into a hotel that smells like washing-up liquid over cleaned-up sick. A stuffy room. Not bright and light, a real contrast to the castle. I've seen it in vision. Temple, castle – call it what you will. Blue and gold painted symbols on the walls. Treehouses and telepathy. No phones allowed, only walkie-talkies. It's some sort of version of paradise, surrounded by English villages and sunny fields.

The cassette is psychoactive. I listen to it over and over and can't get past the fact that it's my own voice being played back to me, yet I have no memory of ever having made the recording.

Three years ago in the London prison, the asymmetric eye.

Bex surfs in different paradigms, speaks in repeated catchphrases and sentences, as though wanting to be remembered and noted. Self-aware enough to know she's a performer in her own narrative, living out her Facebook status, constructing plots and sequences while secretly confident she's being quite influential.

She's flamboyant and funny. A so-called 'leading light' in the movement, who no one takes seriously because of her drug habit.

She staggers in with her banjo. Strums the first few chords of something she's written, then drums the room up into an oi-punk chant.

She'll engage largely via confrontation. It's a trait I've seen deployed by activists elsewhere, though its root cause is different here. Bex is your garden-variety anarchist. Her sexuality is informed by a trauma somewhere deep in her childhood. It has produced a distress pattern and slightly chaotic method of social interaction. Dysfunction round the dinner table, I'd wager. Or possibly being wrongly accused of sexualising a family member.

She was about eleven when the mythology started. A reputation cultivated, which had now stuck. She survives her lifestyle by dipping in and out of various sub-narratives. Online she's prone to playing the role of court jester, often referring to herself as an investigative journalist, raising the spirits with efforts to entertain, and abusing herself badly in the purchase. It's faintly amusing, and painful to watch.

On other occasions she assumes the air of sophisticated upper-class detective. An alter-ego that is suited and booted, her personality entirely dependent on what substances are to hand, and who she is trying to impress.

Today, for some reason, it's me.

On an unconscious level, we've already entered into some sort of agreement. A feeling between us established at the point of eye contact.

Her face has a crater-like surface. A sad, hollow look to her eyes – they appear dark to me in that moment, though weeks later I'll note them down as a definite turquoise.

"You're here to spy on us, aren't ya?" she says.

"But of course."

She nods conclusively, a little nervous at having gotten such a straight answer. I decide to continue using this helpful, therapy-approved persona as it seems to be working.

"Why don't you do something constructive rather than accusing everyone of being a spy all the time?"

"Because I believe you to be an agent of the crown."

Later that night she sits in the shadows at the back, handling the warm crack-pipe. Apparently, she'd started out fairly sane at a tree protest in Devon, but after moving to London had fallen in with the wrong crowd. A rumour started going round about her. Some say it was a story generated by the police to put her name into disrepute, due to the fact she refused to toe the line. Now they say she's an informant working for MI5.

Drank. Seas to cross. Departing from the Hendon shore, with a mouthful of Tricantamin and armed only with a felt-tip pen, a tattooed tooth and flies on my hands. On the other side of slide, I turn and run. The ghost of caffeine in my veins.

I have to look in the mirror, to see if I'm still there.

The drinks trolley goes by, hot chocolate and Genoise sponge cakes are ordered for a heroin addict in withdrawal who works for a broadsheet newspaper.

I later get patronised by a much younger goddess, an aspiring Athena.

The pirate appears. On adventures, he meets with all kinds of dangers. Wizards and shamans, kings and queens that have fallen and turned into crunched-up drug dealers, huffing and puffing in bags. Stolen watches and broken keys. Colourful apples and teeth.

I keep wanting to look behind me as I'm scared again. People seem like pirates – drunk and demented but wearing suits. Trying to get bits of fruit out of plastic cups. Maybe they shouldn't be allowed alcohol. Sneeze.

I've done this before; done it too many times for it to be normal or right. A fit or an allergy to something, not infectious. The horrid trauma-tire. Different versions of self on timeline.

Getting pulled into odd frequencies. Maybe I'll be attracted to New York or possibly Budapest. Follow my feet.

You have to have a few hobbies in life.

I don't know how I keep going.

I'd started a rumour about myself that I was related to a famous icon of the sixties – the girlfriend of an influential rockstar. Soon enough word got round that I'd been brought up in East LA, surrounded by guitars and top-of-the-ladder grass. This was a problem, as I sat in the middle of the settee, a sleeping bag wound round my legs.

Don't want to go back to the protest, that's for sure. Too many people I've just created for the sake of my cover. Oh, you know about the background people. Funny how they do exist.

Gonna leave London. Don't know why, or if it'll work. Surely life could be more chaotic, but I just don't feel like quitting yet. I want to bring these bastards in. I'm going to solve the case of Bex Riley. Missing person since 2023.

It is an old hotel. Seems to have the air of sexual abuse about it. On that first afternoon, a woman sits at the table furthest away from me. She lights up a cigarette and orders something off the à la carte menu.

The sea is the same colour as the eyes of a sickly cat standing in the doorway.

The well-dressed woman is wearing knee-high boots and says she approves of the macaroni. I see her glimpse the tattered Moleskine tucked beneath my palm.

Recruitment

My name is Compost Mckenzie and I worked undercover as a peace activist from 2022 to 2026.

In writing this confession, I hope to expose some of the covert methods by which activists are targeted. Upon publication of this book, I will be free of the lies, duplicity and espionage – but I don't ever expect to be forgiven. Not only did I betray the trust of my comrades, but I deceived family and friends away from the job. For many years my parents believed I was suffering from a personality disorder. As I write this, my transactions are being monitored. My movements carefully tracked.

I was recruited to work for MI5 in the summer of 2021. Much of this account has been written in the third person – this is to distance myself from the altered state I would get into when characterising myself as an activist. I will, for the most part, refer to myself by my nickname, Compost Mckenzie, the name the activists gave me. Eventually, it would become the code name the services would use to refer to me also.

I was an undergraduate at an English conservatoire when my then tutor, Professor Sam Renningstall, took the decision to mentor me.

Recruiting an agent isn't like in the movies. You aren't led to a hotel room and shown a private file they're keeping on you; they don't just give you a card. Blackmail is the easiest way of engaging an asset but also the least effective, as it does not ensure loyalty.

There is another method of recruitment. One that involves the indoctrination of an asset against their will. It is my assertion that many of the individuals working today are not even aware they are deep-cover operatives.

Renningstall organised what I thought was an anarchist working group at a nearby building on the Thames. However, the term 'anarchist' was being misused to describe what was really a hard-left political agenda.

He taught all his students the consensus decision-making technique, and said he had contacts within the entertainment industry. He had also been a professor at two other major universities since the nineties, and I would later learn was a counter-intelligence officer for MI5.

The agency had been careful to create dependency. If I knew then what I know now, I'd have realised that nothing is free and would have been more hesitant before accepting what at the time felt like free help and generosity.

Not long after my first semester, I got appointed adviser on a script that went to a big TV network. I was prompted to drop in casual one-liners about a new vaccine. At the time, I didn't see my work as being part of a political agenda; Renningstall had instilled in me an attitude of assertiveness and certainty and I believed I was behaving with integrity.

In 2026, towards the end of my time with the intelligence services, I would go to see a hypnotist – but by this point doctors were already colluding with police and the results were inconclusive.

I'll admit in the early days the main thing that kept me coming back were the women. I behaved irresponsibly and yet at the time would not have seen my actions as being problematic. Consent was an issue. I was encouraged to have close liaisons with some of the female activists. The details of these affairs have already been extensively covered in the press. This will be my first-hand account of my on/off relationship with Bex Riley, whose loyalty has remained a mystery to me to this day.

The agency had primed me for many years, doing extensive research into my family and university contacts. I later found out they were even working with the modelling agency who scouted me at the Camden Underworld when I was just fifteen.

I still do not know why I was targeted. I know a lot of people won't want to hear that. But uncovering the extent of this intrusion into my personal life has been one of the major incentives behind my wanting to get out. It also goes some way to explaining why I felt at ease and willing to share private information with a sixty-year-old stranger.

Renningstall had programmed me to want to succeed in my career at whatever cost, even brainwashing me into saying I'd do prison time if it came to it. He not only functioned as a mentor, but also occupied the role of father figure.

We became acquainted at a pub on Chancery Lane, where he gained my trust over a period of weeks.

I wasn't surprised to learn he was from a military background. It wouldn't have meant anything to me then. I wasn't connected to any protest groups or anarchist organisations at the time, and had no cause to suspect he would be carrying listening devices.

A vital factor in my recruitment was this sense that I was being invited into a world that felt familiar. He used to drop in casual remarks. Said they'd be there if I needed anything.

Looking back, it all makes perfect sense – that our meetings took place in locations that held a special significance to me. A vegetarian restaurant in Euston that had been a family haunt since my childhood, and the library behind the Royal Courts of Justice, where my father's chinaware dynasty is located.

If anyone ever accused me of being a spy, I would, of course, have denied it – not because I was lying, but because I wasn't consciously aware I was one. Of course, there were indications; coincidences I chose to ignore. And never underestimate the power of denial.

I ought to have noticed the red flags sooner, but my life was made very comfortable by Renningstall and his cohorts. In my second year at drama school, I was transferred from the halls of residence and placed in a flat in South Kensington. I was given membership to the Chelsea Arts Club and encouraged to befriend some of the types that associated there. This was all part of my cultivation into a group, a set – what I thought was a network of actors and writers but turned out to be something much more sinister.

The only person who really knew the truth about me was Bex Riley, the troubled schizophrenic girl with whom I was sent to develop a relationship.

I have sometimes wondered if it's possible she may have functioned in the same capacity as I did, targeting me with her own psychic spying techniques, feeding intelligence back to her private army of anarchist journalists.

My contract with Thayer Holdbrook officially started in 2022. I was asked to take part in a filmed audition for a TV documentary about a riches-to-rags punk band. I was told to play a rebellious eco-warrior and storm off in the middle of the audition. I thought nothing of it and was pleased when they asked me back for a photo shoot the following week. This was to be my first taste of going undercover, though of course I did not know it at the time.

Benefits would include a laptop, iPhone and £800 towards

a new wardrobe. But first I would need to immerse myself in the atmosphere of living in a sustainable community.

I was interested in the opportunity to work overseas; £45,000 per annum wasn't bad and I could look forward to the chance to move to NYC, Melbourne, LA or Singapore. I must admit I felt a little uneasy when I was told I'd be spending time with a group of young anarchists, but thought I'd hold fire and see what the job offered. Apparently, it was all going to be put towards research for an even bigger TV movie where I was up to play the lead.

I was assigned to join an organised group of anarchist activists who specialised in occupying disused tube stations, museums and London Authority buildings. Prep for this was spending two months at a housing co-op in Bristol, getting up to date on all the latest fads and conversation topics, as well as familiarising myself with street banter and what brand of beer to drink.

The agency had me proactively sourcing new clients all the time. Headhunting prospective radicals and feeding back information to the network. What I did not realise is that anyone who needed censoring would be discredited using a mental health diagnosis, following weeks of covert undercover monitoring.

It was part of my job to ascertain the temperature of the more rebellious, free-thinking radicals at the time.

The agency could pick out potential leaders easily as they worked with all the best occultists in the country. If a target was manipulable, they were brought in for a mental health assessment, and offered paid activism as a future career path. Those who'd gone further to decondition themselves were dealt with by other means.

By inflicting mental instability, we could encourage a culture at the same time as creating enough doubt to implode the movement from within. Conversation topics soon turned from coal-seam gas extraction to StingRay surveillance. The aim was to infiltrate a genuine movement, tidy up the revolution, and repackage it back to the mainstream so as to neutralise the threat.

By the time we'd finished with them, our little anarchists couldn't organise a piss-up in a brewery ...

Leytonstone

In Leytonstone they're not awake. Brown carpet, beanbag, things draped over chairs and beer cans strewn everywhere, cigarettes stuffed in them, and joints in the ashtrays.

Looks like it was a good party. Where's that girl with the jet-black hair and red lipstick, slurring her words and wiping snot on her jeans? Compost Mckenzie replays the events of the night before as the coffee starts to unlock his brain.

She'd wanted to move in, but they'd only just met. He too had felt the terror of Woodside Park in the blazing summer. The sad comfort of the urban institution. She used to smuggle wine in. God knows how they got it past the nurses.

My teeth hurt, he thinks. Here, have a handful of drugs. He's taking caffeine tablets disguised as speed, tripping on alcohol and philosophy. Rooftop conversations on other people's income. He wants to go inside the camera.

He walks and walks until he feels himself going into another world. He used to go on these transcendental walks, smoking obsessively and just talking to God.

Well, after a while they caught him.

Stuckley Street, the block of flats opposite Chicken Cottage. Go up in the lift and he answers the door eating a boiled egg, half in his mouth and the other half in his hand. The drag queen welcomes the model in. Says he's gonna do his hair yellow and green. In two hours, he turns you into a vision.

Teeth are baking at the top; dentists refuse the non-fluoridated version. But who can you tell these things to? Not your key worker. We wrote on the back of vans round Lisson Grove, St John's Wood. There were things switching in the walls, no one minded. Or you could go at other odd hours: see snakes, dogs and daggers.

In the second decade of his life, Mckenzie mainly explored the alternative music scene. Industrial and gothic rock, that kind of world.

There was a community: he recognised people as he rode on a top deck at night, looking out the night bus window, catching the 29 past Torriano Avenue on towards where that girl lived, the one who only ate Skittles. Push on 'til five a.m. Spending time sitting cross-legged on carpets in disused office blocks in squats, that's how you'll spend your twenties, I don't think.

When will you learn? says a voice to a person. Learn is earn, if you take the L out of it.

Drank the last of my coffee and felt my teeth move.

He wishes to be in magazines and have affairs with popstars.

Walk to Camden, go on. Even though you're in Wales.

He was glad to get out of the city. Had been in most of the shops by the end of the afternoon. Sliding out of one terminal, past some abandoned car park buildings, all graffiti writing on them.

'Demzcm-demz-enak.tame.' Whatever that means. Thoughts go to things he'd rather not mention. "At least now I know for definite that I don't want to be a professional footballer."

Blah blah blah. This is a boring diary. Mckenzie needs some drugs to bring him to something interesting.

Back to London to Papa John's Pizza delivery bikes and the W17 bus to Leytonstone. Women with washed-out charity shop clothes and receding gums. Those shopping trollies with strawberries printed on them in overly bright colours.

Plastic bottles stuffed between seats. Someone constantly smoking cannabis outside the solicitors. Will it be a quiet road?

Girls try to look older by carrying handbags, but you can tell by their spots. Not too worried about the smoke anymore. And not too worried about money. Thoughts return to the usual escapism. Number 66 to Romford station. It's the time of day when kids play in the street. Boys trying to act tough and then scream away babyishly as they get chased by a wasp.

The inherent aggression of the Central Line. People rushing past on too much cheese. Sleep for breakfast, sleep for supper.

Woke up too early again. A woman with an older face and blue hair. Dots round her lips from too many piercings. Taken out for some job interview, and never put back. 1997. Socks pulled up and that's the end of it. Wonder where she went. How many people round here are originally from Catford.

Land Rover. Jeep.

Gone down spiral after spiral and always come out at Paddington. *'We are breastfeeding welcome.'* People with names like Gareth and Tim grow up expecting (TIME) specifics, but talk about vague.

Will food help? Maybe food will help. Maybe starvation will help – or just not anything in between, like a diet. If certain things are too in balance, then other things get seen, the things we would not show. Observances and awarenesses. Stuff to do with nothing too specific. Liminal spaces of turned-off joy. Oh, you just get too endless in there, talk normally for once, keep it rooftops.

Tea tree bath and kill the warts. A W13 goes by, it's jam-packed. You think about breaking up with Susan.

Now that she don't suffer fools.

Picking her nose and not caring. Staring into the distance. Cared for like there's nothing better to fucking do.

All clothes in a heap, ready for ripping. She never cleaned her underwear, just bought more. The flat was a tip. Porchester Terrace. I moved in there. I mean, Mckenzie moved in there, after the first breakdown. What they termed at the time 'psychosis'. Fresh out the nut ward and back on seven pills a night – but only at weekends. During the week it was just pizza, beer and revision. Exam dissertations between lots and lots of mochas. How can someone from 'old money' turn out so skint? Drinking tomato soup out the tin, get serious. Trying to scare her to make yourself seem tough.

He sits in the car, Twix and melted Maltesers dried into a big gloopish chunk beside his head.

Tastes the same anyway, no it doesn't. Some people don't even bother with sentences, some people don't even bother with words – it's natural and eventual, a response to living in large cities. With no heir.

The Marks and Spencer pantheon was as good a place to start as any. More women with short haircuts reading manufactured journalism. It would do for the time. Of course, most people would expect to see someone of his standing in Liberty's at least. He likes it because it's 'unpretentious.' The lady with the high-waisted slacks and fruity rucksack gets ready to leave. She's probably driving back to Arnos Grove or somewhere – that's been a day out for her. Tea in the M&S on Tottenham Court Road. I'm enjoying a Coke on the firm and thinking about the next six months undercover. It's almost been a year since the dreaded book fair.

The woman with short hair and spangly rucksack walks past again. Mckenzie imagines her having a suburban safe life, which he'd like to share. Of course, he's probably wrong about her. This being only the image she wishes to project. It's too late for me to turn round now, thinks Mckenzie.

For years they'd been living above the HSBC in Holborn. She orders the baked potato with spicy tuna and carries on working.

Notice it's the exact same version of 'rich but casual' she'd been wearing on Monday.

Mckenzie dances with language. Oh, why do I think about Grace and her *fromage frais*? I don't care about what yoghurt you eat, let's be extreme.

He writes a note to say he's saving, starving. Next week he's overspending, stuffing. See, it's all linked.

Says he admires women with dark rings under their eyes who read voraciously. Originally from Devon or Somerset but living in the city and working as an editor. Very good money. Smoker, probably. Goes to galleries and was abused. Yes, that's the sort of woman.

She's got grey hair, and he wonders why she never bothers to dye it. He's addicted to hair dye. This one just lets it frizz and do whatever, she cares not for men, but if she does date them then usually stabs above her weight. She's an over-achiever, an entrepreneur. Living in Forest Gate now, I've heard mention.

You've never even met her, Mckenzie.

If she saw you in Ladbroke Grove again, she'd love to ask, "Can you still afford to live round here?"

These people with their lapdogs, I mean laptops.

Walked there one last time. To celebrate. Remember how far you've come since a year ago. What drive, what stamina you have. And it occurs to him as he walks through the smooth swaying pavements, the spitless streets of Kingsway, that he's spunked all his cash on cabs and cocaine.

Everything he'd earned in his years working for the agency, had gone.

This is the sort of place that pretends to serve food, but the main reason you come here is because of the wine.

There are a few schizophrenics still living in Kilburn. They're few and far between. Have to be really seriously mentally ill, like not washing or able to cook your own meals.

Never really looked at it like that, but in many ways he couldn't stop washing and that's just about the same thing.

'I joined the movement when I was a lapsed Catholic.'

No, scribble it out. It was a silly thing to say.

A Papa John's delivery bike speeds its way through Wanstead high street. He watches the kids crossing the street and thinks very carefully about breakfast.

Women talk seriously over coffee. The man walks his dog. Boy bounces a ball. That fun excited feeling of just getting out of the school gates, the anticipation of sweets from the garage. With friends, magic, leafy. Summer's over. Going back in September. The schoolgirls order individual garlic breads and go and sit on the green.

They're friends but people usually have an agenda.

She's on the veranda. Glass out, next to a Lucozade, unpoured. Her iPad's blaring out something by a pop starlet and she is nodding to the music, long, thin hands with smooth palms which she strokes while she's deciding something.

"What drugs do you do?"

"Everything except crack and smack. You?"

Pharmaceutical drugs. It's just like ecstasy without the buzz. The Tricantamin causes long-term damage to serotonin production – ie, the chemical in the brain that makes you feel natural happiness. What an excellent payoff! Word to the wise. Go easy on the exclamation marks. Don't want to look too excitable or it might look manic.

"Take one." The girl in the bowler hat offers me one of her cigarettes.

Laughing gas canisters round her neck on a chain. Nitrous oxide. "I've been in Vogue," I tell her.

We both look around.

"And now you've been here."

We aren't confined to things like seconds, hours or conventional time. We have odd moments of synchronicity which I treasure but don't trust.

It's a fine face – not exactly pretty, but elegant, handsome. A good jawline and a thick lower lip. Later, after the skin had lost some of its bloom, I noticed the lips go from red to bloodless. The cold took all the colour out of her. Father sucks a Strepsil at the funeral.

The Ghost of Caffeine walks up Harrow Road to get a packet of cigarettes from the petrol station. Lonely figure. Doesn't go out much. Bit of a recluse. They delete my file.

Like every other decision he'd made along the way, Mckenzie's choice to become an activist was due to a dire need for acceptance. A long-term addiction to being liked had put him in some fairly awkward situations. He longed to be respected and use his position to 'make a difference', and during this process had somehow managed to offend almost everyone he'd come into contact with. It was a perverse mystery to the aspiring anarchist, who viewed himself as an open-minded and honourable individual.

British intelligence agencies are not obliged to confirm or deny who works for them.

Bizarrely enough, this one had come up through the industrial music scene, to which MI5 regularly supplied creative informants. Infiltrating the subculture was a vital way of dripfeeding spies back into the network. A tendency to sniff out subversives was what had first put him on their radar, and yet Mckenzie wasn't involved in any of the groups. Surprisingly, he actually went to gigs for the music.

Bex was cold, brazen and a liar; it was part of what made her so magnetic to secret police, ie, social justice warriors. Being what you might call a shy extrovert, Mckenzie was able to maintain a level of political neutrality whilst coaxing his friends into revealing their true nature.

The Lies and Tells of Compost Mckenzie wants to be written. It rests in the hands of a man in his late twenties, who undoes the twine on the empty notebook and begins to fondle his pen.

He does not have a name for the main character.

'Names are not important,' he writes. *'I am the legal inhabitant of that name.'* He surrounds the sentence in a childish speech-bubble.

Sometimes he hears his thoughts narrated to him in other accents, a voice that is not his own. Today it's Southern Irish. Why does he get the word 'Glasnevin'?

Later that night he'll watch a TV show and an actor with that exact same voice will be on screen speaking.

Mckenzie often gets voices in his head; however, at this point in time he has no way of knowing that other people don't experience these things, and so doesn't think of it as special or odd.

The group are sitting in a pub near the college but away from the main table where the popular kids are talking. Stupid shallow crap that doesn't interest him. He wants to go out and get galaxy-brained with the punk girl from the protest. Bex is dangerous, bolshy and a bit older. She has been known to put out rumours about herself that she's an informant, but of course this isn't true.

Bex isn't together enough to be a spy. Anyone can see that. She's the sort of girl to level you in an argument; a boisterous bully with a tendency to talk over people and sing drunk in shop doorways.

I would not be alive today were it not for that woman, he thinks solemnly. They'll first meet in an addictions clinic, but it won't be until later, during his first undercover assignment, that they will become what you might call friends.

Of course, she knows who he is, what he does; but they are able to communicate on the basis that in a strange sort of way, they are playing the same game.

The squares from the modelling agency go out drinking and end up at some cheesy place in Leicester Square. They always invite him, but Mckenzie isn't interested. He wants to be part of the elite bunch of anarchist squatters that run with Bex's crew.

He sits in front of the computer screen and opens up the web browser. He's hoping for a few more comments on his blog, which covers the high-profile occupation of the Port of London Authority building, but instead sees an email from a name he does not recognise. He has to type it into a search engine after he reads the long-winded, slightly chaotic email – as he can't for the life of him recall who 'Harry Pothead' is. He quickly goes through a mental filing-cabinet of all the people he might have met with that name. Straight away he gets a mental image of a short man gyrating to "Tipsy" by J-Kwon at the student bar in 2019. Harry had been a good dancer. Some might even say professional.

Biro

It must have started that afternoon when I went out to France to buy a biro. I knew how to get money, that wasn't a problem. But it was more a case of doing it ethically and not leaving a trail of evidence in my wake. It was decided that 6 a.m. was generally a good hour for me to rise. My handlers imposed themselves upon virtually every aspect of my life, and I trusted them completely.

When I needed to tune in to Mckenzie, I simply changed the font on my laptop from Comic Sans to Courier. Obviously not all of us had that luxury, but MI5 had built my computer.

I realised early on that the people who busied themselves with meetings and tech tents were up to no good. We've driven back to Camp Hamlin, the frack site that borders London.

It always seems to be sunny there. The campsite next to the drill rig feels more like a festival. The sky is so blue it's stifling. We are welcomed with hugs and given clean sleeping bags. Led to our familiar sleep-space, a couple of hay bales in the geodesic dome. It's warm and the air is clear and sweet. I wonder how long we'll be allowed to stay here this time. Please let it be longer.

There are treehouses decked out with rainbow bunting and swings built out of old tyres drawn across the dell that leads to a lake. The fracktivists have made it into their own adventure playground. People commune round fires, chatting and sharing smoke while pretty girls hula-hoop in the dwindling sunlight. The sweet scent of hashish permeates the cool evening air as a tray of hot beverages gets handed round.

It is then that the realisation descends upon me. I am not one of these people. I am here to bring this lovely happy pirate playground to a close.

A chap calling himself Evil Rick has come over to wash his hands.

"Been over at duck-shit lake. You got a razor?"

"No, I don't carry one." I tell him. He surveys my ginger beard.

"What's your name, laddie?"

He knows my name but is perhaps trying to assert his dominance by pretending it's slipped his mind. He's using his large stature to intimidate me. I won't buck. I'm simply not the sort of person who supplies razors to fracktivists.

Bex is sleazing around in the kitchen. Anarchists tend to think differently, they are able to discern things about themselves. Perhaps it's the group-soul that has taken me over recently, an altered state one gets into after hanging out with people with shared beliefs. A lithe-looking fellow is standing by the geodesic dome talking about ancient civilisations and at the same time showing a group of people how to tie a knot.

I can discover very complex subjects, and am a critical thinker, but cannot do simple funny things like make paper airplanes. Knot-tier guy is encouraging and kind and seems eager to put across the point that no one will judge us here.

There's something about him that makes people listen. It's not because he's trying to convince anyone of anything, it's just the way he's so inclusive, even of himself.

His name is Jarod, and he tells me he never takes part in meetings, or if he does, is usually somewhere laying on his back. I appreciate that his initial sternness may have been down to him being one of the initiators who set up the camp, and he's therefore protective of it.

"We just don't wanna risk it getting infiltrated by cops again," he confides, handing me an oat-milk mocha with chocolate sprinkles. I put down my wooden bowl of stew, I'm certainly getting well-fed here. The main thing I notice is how different the atmosphere is when there's no alcohol around.

The meetings are made up of self-confident neurotypicals with careers ahead of them and a PhD. And the Jarods of this world. Invincibly unemployable and with an ability to formulate ideas and counterarguments.

It's the 23rd of September again and I can't help pondering on the significance of that number, how it keeps synchronistically occurring.

I walk down to the village pub and who should be there but the two spies from Nanowore. They're sitting there with full English platters, swilling lattes. All their tech equipment sprawled out on the table, hooked up to wires. They greet me enthusiastically, but I can detect from their initial note of panic that they're unprepared to see me.

Organised brands like the one they're part of do not interest me. A group is not a community. Most of the individuals who gravitate towards the highly structured environments are already more than willing to give their freedom away in exchange for a few hours of 'activism'; it gives them a sense of comfort, makes them feel virtuous, like they're doing something.

But these new camps across the country are a real cause for concern. The tribe is complex. Well-meaning students and pop stars' kids are getting involved. Its highly possible Special Branch have decided to work alongside a leading news publication and get them out of favour with a new generation of eco-warriors.

Four hours have passed.

I haven't lost control and stand there generalising from his haircut. Evil Rick strikes me as someone who must have a vice. Doesn't drink and hasn't got a partner. There's something else underneath. What is it? A desire for reckless gay abandon in the woods.

A helicopter goes over and hovers just above us, purring violently for a sec, then swerves off towards the drill rig.

I talk to Bex in my head, then prepare a walk-on sentence.

The usual trajectory of conversation transpires. Memorised sentences featuring quoted statistics. I want to probe a bit further; see what this one knows.

We're all sitting round discussing the media training workshops and how useful (useless) they can be.

"When someone asks you a difficult question, you say, 'that's a really good question', which gives you time to think," Rick tells me.

"Ever wonder who brings in all that good food and pays to have a chef installed?" says Bex.

"Who cares?"

It's the first time I've seen him speak his mind. For a split second he looks like he wants to apologise, but I shush him and nod, as if to say, no, that's good, please continue.

The rest of the time it is not his mind, but the words he has memorised to say in order to gain respect and acceptance among his peers.

There's a moment when Bex strays to more controversial strategies, describing badger traps and a charge of criminal damage, which seems to get everyone excited. I can tell that she's already rebelling against the formula of organised protest and is ready to be brought on board.

Years ago, we had come here to discuss a cause. We remembered to say words in the right order, things that could describe a process that would lead to massive disruption of the planet, but words like 'environment' had come to be associated with certain thresholds of boredom.

I decide to go back to the camp. Sianne is there, she only ever seems to hang out with the older women. They protect her like Christianity's hidden goddess.

As long as we have the bullies, our operation is stable. There are a lot of people out here – healers, herbalists. People who live off-grid.

A car with blacked-out windows pulls up round the back of the tents and delivers a crate of wine. There are fires lining the side of the road, little divisions.

At the pub, I stare off into the distance as Bex gets the beers in. She's humming along to an indie-pop track that's playing in the background. Sky News is showing the same bulletin on repeat of a copper who got murdered outside Highbury and Islington tube station. The barman hums and stares past the screen, not consciously aware of the imagery. Police in riot gear shown parading outside a well-known venue in Oxford Street, as the column of red text underneath continues to feed an array of devastating headlines. That night I have a dream about saucepans.

Party

I spend a long time trying to pick what brand of beer to bring. They'll laugh if I get Fosters and call me lightweight. Stella is too middle class, and cider looks like you're trying too hard. Finally, I decide on a bottle of cheap wine and a crate of Red Stripe, the beer I've seen Bex drinking in a few of her Facebook photos.

I wonder whether to bring someone with me to the party and half-heartedly scroll through the list of contacts on my mobile phone. In some ways I don't trust my utopian choice of drinking partners.

There are a few from my drama school days. Jamie Cokes, the cider-drinking playwright from first year – he's actually doing too well to attend. And then there's Bourcier; unlikely to make it – he has proper priorities, like experimenting with LSD and reading William Faulkner novels in pubs alone around Putney.

I think forward to the night ahead, anticipating the glitterati of the London protest circuit: the army of ravers, rentboys, drop-outs and freeloaders. An assortment of bohemians and weirdos who each fit into their category and have their stereotype to live up to.

Getting ready in front of the full-length gold gilt mirror, I imagine it is going to be the sort of place I'll make some fairly important connections. I adjust my designer cardigan and try on a different pair of boots. The hairstyle isn't working, I want to look less like I've tried to style it.

An hour later, I make my way to the tube station.

They are slowly turning up the volume on the announcements – I am sure of it. But you say things like that to people and they look at you as though you're crazy.

The grey and brown interior of a Bakerloo line train is always pleasantly familiar. It is odd how each station has its own smell. The Bakerloo line has a warmed-up school-halls smell that hits you as soon as you descend the steep stone steps.

I notice a fresh batch of SWP stickers. They've been cropping up everywhere recently, something to do with Comrade Delta.

A grumpy old woman with a meaty pale face and white hair has pushed in front of me in the queue.

When I arrive, Jarod is organising leaflets by the tea tent. He is clearly only here to get his end away and chat up some of the hunt sabs. Bex is especially drawn to provoking them, and seems to have targeted Tad Hern, a diminutive goth with bad acne and a speech impediment. She starts the conversation by hurling moral judgements at the tea lady, Arna. This seems to enrage Jarod, who won't stand for bullying of any sort.

I sip my coffee, eager to look like I don't want to fit in.

"Almond or cow?" Jarod asks.

Very early on in my career as an activist, I become aware of an ongoing source of contention. Milk. Soya, almond, semi-skimmed ... I'd witnessed many heated debates about this matter and had concluded that it in fact had very little to do with dairy and really seemed to be an opportunity for people to project their childhood traumas onto each other.

To be on the safe side, I opt for almond. Jarod seems to approve of this and warmly offers me a plate of biscuits.

A lot more people are arriving. I recognise some of the older activists from previous incarnations and take up residence in the tea tent next to Bex Riley. I try to approach her from round the central table where Evil Rick is neurotically arranging flyers. I decide to drop something in about the illegal eviction.

"What are your views on the arrests yesterday?"

"Fucked if I know," she says simply.

I try and steer the conversation towards something that will interest her.

"Did Rob Dawlish ever stop working for MI5?"

Small talk is not my strong point. Most intelligence gatherers are good at sticking to the script, but I struggle with timing.

I try and find my angle into the conversation and feel like I'm wearing a name tag.

Arna is keen to get the water boiled and asks me what I think about the injunction. I say I'm not legally allowed to speak about it.

"See you at four p.m. in the tea tent," she says, giving me a knowing nod. "We're doing a workshop on face recognition and CCTV."

Pass me the broccoli, Your Majesty.

Later that evening, I stand in the doorway, choosing what aftershave to wear. I know Bex doesn't care for perfume, she prefers natural smells.

I douse myself in Rose Maroc and hope for the best.

We stand outside. I can see Jarod is struggling. Not as confident as the others. Probably was unpopular at school and found his niche here among the outcasts. Social hierarchy is important to him, but he tries too hard.

He talks to his girlfriend. They're in love, you can tell – which is unfashionable in relationship anarchy circles. Given time I'll remove the trust that seems so peaceable between them.

Dinner is a plate of breadsticks and six cans of supermarket own-brand lager. I hand Sianne a stolen bottle of wine and she gives me the double thumbs-up.

I listen to her talk about Snowden. She's posh mixed with common, peppered with interesting aphorisms. Boarding school survivor. Her attempts to run away were never meant to be successful; she did it more as a demonstration than anything else. She's pretty damned attractive, if you must know. Wide-set blue eyes in a young, malnourished face. Tie-dye shawl round dirty loose-slung jeans.

"We're watching *Citizenfour* on the projector tonight."

The event is all part of what some people are referring to as the 'Langton Occupation'. Former Port of London Authority building.

Another journalist has arrived. She sits on an upturned beer crate.

"That Jenny Balstamp is upstairs apparently."

"Here to promote her new book," I say cynically.

"What's it like living here?"

I size her up. Miss Prissy. Lips outlined correctly in pillar-box red. A reject from *UK's Next Top Model*. This one has a habit of closing her eyes in concentration when other people are speaking. She'd been in last week, flouncing about in a fake fur shawl, all green and cream lace. Couldn't miss her.

"Oh, it's a breeze; I adore anarchy." I'm feeling facetious and I don't know why. Could be Bex's influence rubbing off on me.

Miss Prissy is carrying a flesh-coloured handbag that looks designer, a broken strap linked by a makeshift carabiner.

With a hint of anger, I plonk myself down on the sofa next to her. She nods approvingly.

"Good book?"

I look up through two greasy tendrils of bleached blond hair.

"It was just on the table."

"I know – it's mine," she says.

"Oh, sorry."

"That's OK, you'll do."

I feel my anaemic features crease into a smile, giving me a double chin.

"Are you a smoker?" I ask, delicately reaching into my coat pocket to grab one of the cigarette props.

"Why sure," she says, oozing sass and fake politeness.

She produces a lighter from her coat pocket, and, taking the cue, leans in, making sure to look up at me as she takes her first inhalation.

She's flirting. I shrug this off. Giving a baffled shake of the head, I begin my interrogation.

Her life story comes across like a PowerPoint presentation with BDSM themes – not that I'm complaining. I tell her half-exaggerated truths and for some reason share a story about me snorting vodka backstage at a Cradle of Filth concert.

There's the sound of nervous laughter at the space between conversation as we become aware of mutual attraction.

"What are we doing then?" she finally asks me.

"I haven't got any life plans beyond next weekend," I admit, demolishing the end of an Aero in one mouthful. "There's that fancy-dress party at Evil Rick's later …"

"That would be alright, it's not too far from here."

"But I've got a few deliveries to make first."

"Fine."

I feel myself relax, safe in the knowledge that drugs will be in no short supply for the remainder of the weekend.

I'm thinking about her body. Quite masculine, with broad shoulders and a boyish frame. She's not wearing tights and has on a short rubber miniskirt.

I notice her legs are unshaved and feel aggravated by this act of self-assertion.

She has a loud, entitled way of speaking, which has me on edge from the get-go.

I imagine nice bedsheets. Satin, pinky.

"Did you ever watch *The X-Files*?" she says unexpectedly.

"No. People talked about it but I never watched it." I'm not even sure why I'm lying. She laughs and says it must be an age thing. She wants to bring up a picture on her iPhone so that she can show me a photo of the female lead. But the real reason is so that I can see her male counterpart, Mulder. Perhaps she thinks it will look good if I dress up as someone else.

We start discussing different people she could go as. She's unconsciously striving for my approval with her suggestions, and I find this deeply off-putting.

I've started talking a bit like the TV detective I'm supposed to be unaware of, affecting these little Mulderisms.

"My friend Clara went as the Joker from *Batman*," she says. "Or was it her girlfriend? I think they both went as him."

"Sounds like she's got it all sewn up."

I want her to tell me I'd look good in a suit, but she's not getting the hint.

"I could eat loads of clotted cream and get plump to look like Marilyn Monroe!"

"But that might affect your health."

"And possibly my sex life …"

I laugh, a sleazy laugh.

This is a transaction; I'll do this if you do that.

"Sometimes it's good for people to mix up cultures. I have two groups of friends."

She then tells me that in the village where she grew up there was a definite point where she rebelled and chose to go round to parties at the flats, instead of just sitting in and staying with her friends.

"It is my highest ambition in life to go and work for Nanowore," she says.

"Where did you grow up?"

"Just outside Hastings. People who move there think it's all nice houses, not realising it's full of bedsits and people living below the poverty line. You know, like, we have a BHS instead of a John Lewis, and the staff who work there don't make as much of an effort as they do in London."

The morning after, we sit drinking coffee in a cheap café. There's no conversation between us really, she doesn't seem to have anything to say. I keep looking out of the window next to her.

I recognise a few faces. The boy who works in Co-op with the lip ring. The odd gay couple who live at the end of the road – the tall one who now has blond hair extensions, and the short one who looks like the guy from Emperor Hawk Moth.

He actually is the guy from the Emperor Hawk Moth. I can't remember who told me that in the midst of drunk confidence.

She tells me she's a novelist and her work is actually published. Before leaving to go to work she gives me a hug and says I can keep her hoodie, which I'm still wearing.

It's soft on the inside; hasn't gotten to that bobbly stage yet.

As she's leaving, she trips over a fire extinguisher, apologises and says, "I'm not an anarchist."

I make a noise to express disappointment.

"Well, I am really," she says, changing her mind to better fit what she thinks I want.

It's 9:59 and life has no meaning. I've been cold all through the night, crouched under a tiny thin duvet.

I'm sure I can hear someone moving around outside on the landing. The shuffling of feet on carpet as I awake suddenly. A scuffling sound, like someone moving the garbage bags from the front door and down onto the fire escape.

Someone going through the trash again. All they'll find is shredded mackerel and stinking rotting yoghurt pots. I know better than to leave hard copies of my communiqués out by the bins.

That night I go upstairs to use the toilet for the sixteenth time.

The tea tent is a warm, bright space, buzzing with spirit. Fairy lights hung over bicycles and plants draped over surfaces, twizzling cocktail glasses on red-painted shelves. Next door to a guitar-grotto. Full studio, drum kit, harmonium. Soft lighting and multicoloured carpets overlapping the floor. The radio is playing softly, 'Dry the Rain' by Beta Band. I pour myself a glass of municipal tap water and stand in the centre of the kitchen. Alex Dubois and Shandy Tomlin have fallen asleep on the sofa, and I can hear the light summer rain outside, hitting the glass of the skylight.

I skin up shakily. I've got a virus knocking round my head which has migrated from my neck to my ears. Living like this is taking its toll. I'm beginning to get a rash. My clothes don't fit me.

Quartz Ward

On Level 1 of the Petersham Building, Bex presses the green entry button on the scuffed metallic panel and waits for the buzzer to sound.

She's already late, but decides to go to the toilet, more out of habit than actual need. Using the pink soap to wash her hands, she reaches for one of the rolled-up flannels stashed in a basket beneath the basin, and as she's drying them, glimpses the bumpy skin beneath her shirtsleeve. Red scabs are beginning to crust along her arm from where she attacked it with a razor blade two weeks ago. The limb itself looks all busted up. She prods at it curiously, at once horrified and adrenalised by her own handiwork.

The main reception desk is manned by an elderly black woman with grey hair. On the wall behind her is a row of certificates, framed and mounted, and beneath them a shelf with a phone and some files. Every door is shut and there's a green button on the wall which unlocks the entry system. Beyond that, a corridor goes out to a hall of dormitories.

Bex is used to making trips to St Pancras, where she was first registered as an outpatient six years ago.

"Hi there," she says. "I've got an appointment at one thirty."

"Witch doctor?"

Bex smiles at the accidental wordplay. These days she can't tell if her thoughts are her own or involuntary responses to the medication she's been taking. It's as though she's inhabiting two worlds. One in which the answer to all her problems is being subconsciously suggested through codes in language, double meanings, signs and coincidences.

"I don't know, she didn't say …" She answers slowly, as though piecing together what all this is really about.

She turns and leans back against the reception desk, surveying the room.

Several green upholstered chairs have been positioned round a small coffee table displaying newspapers and women's magazines.

At the base of the staircase sits a large potted plant with stones instead of soil. There are several tables, and a vase of flowers has been placed on top of each. Patients' artwork is stuck to the beige walls, between two candelabras with fake fire. Below them is a vending machine. Bex helps herself to a coffee.

The receptionist presses something on the computer keyboard and doesn't look up.

"Dr Cruci. Room 47, you can go up," she says, and motions towards the stairs.

The new consultant psychiatrist is still familiarising herself with the file on Bex Riley, a paranoid schizophrenic who has recently been placed under her supervision on Quartz Ward.

"Right, where are we?" Cruci begins. "I can see an initial diagnosis of ADHD and borderline personality disorder …"

She scrolls through the notes and Bex sits cross-legged, awaiting the usual line of questioning.

"Born December 1995 – meaning you'd have been a year younger than the rest of the children in your class?"

"Yeah, I suppose so."

"And you were also diagnosed with oppositional defiant disorder."

"Initially. The army wouldn't let me join because of my depression. They later changed it to bipolar, but by then I had a different doctor."

"And an updated DSM …" says Dr Cruci.

"Can I have one?" says Bex, pointing to the tube of extra strong mints on the desk beside the doctor's handbag.

"Certainly."

Bex reaches over, takes out a mint and pops it into her mouth. She uses her tongue to rotate the powdery lozenge a few times, enjoying the mixture of sugar and spit.

"I've been on loads of medication," she says. "The only one that seems to work is the Tricantamin. That Dwyerbinthol made me froth at the mouth. And it made my breasts lactate."

Dr Cruci nods appreciatively, then turns away from the screen.

"It says here you suffer from psychotic episodes. You believe you are being followed by agents of the British state?"

She speaks without moving her body, her head tilted slightly to one side.

Bex bites into her mint.

"It would probably be rude to ask, but what are the chances of an involuntary sectioning?"

Dr Cruci smiles diplomatically. She has a sloping face. It looks as though she may have had a stroke at some point, or been paralysed by a vaccine.

"You know as well as I do, we can't keep you in unless you're a danger to yourself and others. You'll be asked to attend therapy here with me each Tuesday. It's important that you attend these sessions, or you'll lose your entitlement to your DLA."

Bex is well aware of the procedure. The team at St Pancras just need to show they've done due diligence. Psychiatrists didn't wear uniforms, but their work was still politically motivated.

At least they'd done away with the formalities. No desk, no potted plant, no folder. Just a good old-fashioned database, stored on a computer that anyone could access – or hack.

"Just one question, Bex."

"Yeah?"

"Why would anyone want to follow you?"

Being cross-examined by the security services is like climbing a tree. You have to think twice about your every move.

"Well, I've been attending a protest which is heavily infiltrated, and I suppose you could say I'm quite influential."

Dr Cruci smiles, adept at masking her impatience during what she perceives to be slightly staged moments of crisis. Most of her clients found it difficult to verbalise their phobias, but this one suffered from persistent fixed delusions.

From out the window, an airplane tears the sky, leaving a thick white chemtrail in its path.

During a one-on-one therapy session, the psychiatrist has to enquire as to a patient's progress in recovery, particularly in relation to sleep patterns and personal hygiene. This is to assess whether they can live independently or will need a keyworker assigned.

"I want us to start looking at things in your environment that make you feel good. Think of it as a feel-good scavenger hunt."

Bex thinks of the camera hidden inside the eye of the ONE LOVE Bob Marley poster hanging on the wall of Jarod's flat but decides not to say anything.

"It's all the fault of that Himesh Vianney, if you ask me. He's the real reason I'm here."

Cruci makes a note of the name.

"Is that a boyfriend or something?"

"God no – he's the one targeting me."

"Then why is he listed as your next of kin?"

Bex frowns, unsure if she's being asked a trick question. Then decides she most definitely is.

"It's a long story."

Dr Cruci turns back to her screen. Bex knows her medical file reveals a history of mental illness spanning back nearly a decade.

"What was your favourite game as a child?"

Swiftly the thought goes through Bex's head that Dr Cruci is being prompted by a device inserted into her ear, being made to ask leading questions. They may want to dwell on certain subjects to see how much she knows.

Play it down, she thinks. Don't act mad.

"Hide and seek," she says hesitantly.

The doctor sits back and reflects on this philosophically.

"Some people never stop playing hide and seek their whole lives."

It's a good approach. Feels like more of a conversation than an interrogation. Bex decides she'll play along for a bit.

"I used to like the fantasy stuff. Creating a secret life for myself, hallucinating conversations."

The doctor stops her.

"'Hallucinating' is a very strong word, a rather punishing word. Why don't we try 'imagining'?"

"Yeah, okay. Imagining. I'm not doing that now, though."

Again, Cruci writes something down in her notepad.

"It's really unsettling the way you write everything down. Do you have to?"

"Sorry – I'll stop if you'd rather," she says, putting down her pen. "What did you think when I was writing stuff down?"

Bex takes a long pause as a way of regaining her power,

scolding herself for being temporarily taken in by what is, of course, only professional friendliness.

"It's not about what I think. It's to do with the feelings that come up when you do it. I get extremely anxious."

Cruci nods and glances at the clock.

"What drugs do you do, Bex?"

"Everything except crack and smack. You?"

The doctor ignores her.

"I went through a skipping-rope phase as well, but that was when I was much younger."

"Now you're being passive-aggressive."

"What? No," she says, shaking her head as if to say she does not have time for this. "Can't you stop me going back to the protest? Bail conditions or something? What about the arrest?"

"The arrest didn't take place at the protest site, so you can't be bailed from there. I'm afraid that is a police matter. There's nothing else I can do. I'll prescribe Tricantamin and Dwyerbinthol on a PRM basis and we'll assess again in a month's time. I'll need you to sign these for me," she says, handing her the old-fashioned release form. The physicality of the cardboard at least gives the illusion of respectability.

There's a swell of relief as the interview is terminated.

Stakeknife

Bex sits in the smoking room, feeling invaded after her psychiatric assessment.

She looks up from the book she's reading, a biography of Stakeknife, and glares hopefully at a tray of biscuits being brought in by the nurse.

Being an outpatient on Quartz Ward means crossing paths with the occasional celebrity. A well-known public figure has arrived on the addictions ward. The failed popstar and out-of-work actor has come to the smoking room, which is shared with some of the inpatients. Compost Mckenzie clocks the girl at the back and wonders if he'll be recognised.

Bex likes skinny men with emotional problems and long hair. A fan of indie-rock music, she instantly recognises the smack addict from the papers, and motions for him to come and sit next to her. He approaches.

She doesn't get up but greets him warmly.

"So, you're the famous Compost Mckenzie?"

Usually, people don't acknowledge him so directly. Her audacity puts him at ease.

He's wearing a knot of red and black beads around his wrist. *Abrus precatorius*, the rosary pea; poisonous if it comes into contact with water. Popular among kids into the New Age movement. Gifted to him by a jealous ex-partner, she imagines. Someone into power.

His pink silk shirt is undone to reveal the edge of a colourful statement tattoo. She smirks at this inwardly. Though beguiled by his status, she's immediately cynical of anyone in the public eye who courts the lower classes. From what she's read about him, Mckenzie's a trust fund kid and an occasional eco-activist. She scans his body.

"I approve of the beads. Anarchist?"

"Yeah."

Bex readjusts her bowler hat. Round her neck she has tied a couple of nitrous oxide canisters to a bit of blue string.

"I like your hat," says Mckenzie.

She gives him a withering look. Reaching into her bag, she takes out an engraved chrome zippo lighter and flicks open the cap. She uses it to ignite one of the Chessington cigarettes she keeps stashed in her coat pocket.

"What's your relationship like with the security industry?" she asks, exhaling a ribbon of smoke.

He notices dark circles under her eyes. Skin the texture of plasticine, weathered from alcohol and medication.

"I'm not sure what you're talking about," he says politely. "What are you in here for?"

"Shoplifting, mainly. We got caught in House of Fraser; they have the real-time cameras. Got sent down for six months and they referred me here. Thought they'd throw the book at me."

Two laughter lines sweep the sides of her nose and down to the corners of her mouth, but it's not a healthy smile, more of a grimace really.

"Can I ask what you were stealing?"

"You just did. Pastry forks."

"Pastry forks. Really?"

"No," she laughs.

He smiles nervously. If a woman shows signs of being assertive, he immediately puts her on a pedestal. The fact that she's admitted to being a petty criminal has sullied his image of her, but also increased her credibility factor.

"What are you in here for, really?"

"Oh, purely for journalistic purposes." She smiles. "This year the DSM were offering a new criterion for the personality disorders. Thought I'd take part in the medical trials – for a laugh."

"Personality disorder, is that … what you've got?"

A movement goes across her face. She leans in closer so he can smell the mixture of last night's beer and cigarette-spit.

"Come in here for depression, they treat you with Tricantamin, which has sleeplessness as one of the side effects. So, they give you Dwyerbinthol pills – which induce actual psychosis. Suicide pills, I call them."

She smiles to reveal the discoloured teeth of a junkie.

"Are you on suicide watch?" he asks impulsively.

"Ask a better question."

Dark Day

Dr Cruci is writing up her notes from this afternoon. She occasionally sprinkles them with her own insights, hoping it'll catch the attention of one of the clinicians who sometimes request papers for research. All patients are warned that their notes are confidential unless there is a legal requirement to disclose them under the Terrorism Act.

This twenty-eight-year-old was referred for assessment by the St Pancras mental health team on 23 March. I could elicit delusions of persecution. Ms Riley asked me if I was taping the conversation. She was looking at the walls to see if there were any bugs. She said she is being targeted by the British State because she is a whistle-blower. When I asked her about this, she became guarded and suspicious. She described seeing 'government spies' and 'secret servicemen' around Parliament Square. These were felt to be pseudo-hallucinations.

Ms Riley does not watch television as she is afraid her brain would be interfered with. She feels that her life is being controlled and that her mobile phone is being monitored.

Past psychiatric history shows psychotic behaviour. In view of her paranoid state, she was commenced on Tricantamin 200mg, describing her mood as elated, saying to the admitting doctor, "I feel absolutely fantastic." She was also assessed by Dr Tarable at Woodfield Road, who felt that a diagnosis of paranoid schizophrenia was possible. Riley has used illicit drugs in the past. She denied use of crack cocaine for one month prior to admission, cannabis and ketamine. She smokes 8–10 cigarettes a day.

She should be under long-term psychiatric care.

Dark day in Paddington. A cat runs along the edge of the allotment at Forty-Tree Green, its fur the same colour as the bricks on the avenue, eyes reflecting the pale bark on the Maida Vale conifers.

A bench of that same faded grey stands camouflaged against the empty park.

Cooking smells waft over from a council block. The clatter of cutlery. Boarded-up property with whitewash and writing over it. 'PROTEST ON SUNDAY: SAVE OUR LOVELY PUB.'

A number 6 bus goes by. Then a number 31. Wishy-washy voices and loud alarming announcements – countered by good quality headphones.

The cat with the blond eyes scales the back fence and hops over into one of the adjacent gardens.

Smooth clean pavements. No spit, no gum, no litter. Not like the overflowing plant pots of Pimlico.

Someone on a mobile phone, their voice high-pitched, is cutting into her skull. Bex feels the nerves in the back of her neck sparking and imagines grabbing the phone off the woman and beating her face in repeatedly with the handset. Tricantamin withdrawal has made the rages worse, and she doesn't get her script until Tuesday.

Striding along the side street up towards Delaware Road, she feels her bladder like a solid pellet in her body and gets a flash of it being removed with a pair of pincers, extracted and replaced by something smooth and flat-sided, closely resembling a SIM card.

A van goes past with oversized children's toys tied to the front bars, reminiscent of sinister funfairs.

The veins in the corner of her temple are rippling as a group of schoolkids walk single file along the balcony to number 15.

There's a bit of writing on the corner of the old hotel. 'Fuck the EDL.' The work of a social agitator, or a genuine supporter? She suspected such countersurveillance in the area.

The 'Ban Far Left Fascism' stickers had started appearing several months ago, just before the occupation.

First there'd been messages written in magic marker on the disused telephone boxes near Royal Oak station. Someone trying to get a rise, perhaps. Or could be Special Branch had sent someone down to spook her. Someone who knew her regular route.

Bex knows she's being followed, but the stereotype of a mentally ill person serves as a perfect cover story for her research. A fitting double-bluff that the healthcare professionals see as paranoid delusion. Her mischievous role-playing game has resulted in unintended manifestation.

Harassment tactics had started with visits to the anarchist HQ. Papers going missing, emails disappearing. People contacting her via an old Yahoo account. Upon arrival, it's clear that a documentary being made about their protest is government funded. She has swiftly ascertained that the whole thing has been carefully orchestrated with a safe house serving as a front for one big surveillance operation. Anyone who blows the whistle will be smeared as an agent provocateur.

Helicopters

The texture of the wallpaper looks like dried rice pudding. Bex is bored and wants to fuck Jarod's life up.

How had he gone from being alright company to a walking MK Ultra experiment? It just showed how effective the animal oracle training had been.

It seemed rational to assume that the Langton occupation was the subject of an ongoing inquiry. With Himesh Vianney at the helm, running his clowning workshops and unwittingly training the new kids to be MI5 mind-control spies.

She kicks Jarod's sleeping bag with her boot to see if he's still awake. He groans.

"I don't think Vianney was in on it. Although he wasn't at the Occupied Fish, to be fair."

The others are tired of hearing about her recent victory over Himesh Vianney. Her boasting about it is what gives the game away, the tendency to exaggerate a little too often, and to the wrong people. A few of them think she's a shill; but mostly they don't take her seriously. It didn't help that she'd recently chosen to accept a caution, rather than go to court like the rest of them.

"Yeah, I knew Crowbar Jenkins could be relied on," she says, wiping some snot on her leggings. "Sweet guy. Wouldn't harm a fly. He taught me how to dig a tunnel with a biscuit-tin lid, we were more like brother and sister really."

The sun shines down forcefully through the double-glazed window. Jarod is half asleep now. He's been out all night getting shafted by middle-aged businessmen. When he's getting screwed, he likes to imagine he's the girl from the Pleiadian Vengeance video. When he wakes up, it's usually to the sound of Bex prattling on about the halcyon days of Cordelia Ridge, or her times with the activist Crowbar Jenkins. Sometimes he thinks she might be genuinely brain-damaged from all the Tricantamin she's been taking.

"Those twats at the student demo aren't risking a prison sentence if they get nicked – I am," she says. "It's just another fad for them. Something to pass the time before getting onto a PhD."

Perhaps it frightened his friend to think of herself as someone who'd fallen through the cracks of society. Instead, she tells people she chooses to live outside the system. Bex isn't homeless, she's a gypsy. Her refusal to rent property is a political statement.

She sparks up her morning spliff and takes a sip from her one-litre bottle of Lucozade Energy Original.

She doesn't eat breakfast; food makes her feel ill in the morning.

Propped up in her sleeping bag, she sits reading the latest on yesterday's demo, scrolling down on the iPad, back hunched, looking at the coverage.

"Gimme some of that," says Jarod, grabbing the spliff off her.

Bex scowls. The intention had never been to get him hooked on her best supply. Next time he's round, she'll make sure she's smoking some of that paranoid shit.

Putting mass-produced stickers on lampposts and writing slogans on the backs of toilet doors was all very well, but it wasn't enough. They'd soon need to ramp up their tactics to provide more direct provocation.

"I dunno, they seem well-intentioned enough."

"Look at this ad," says Bex. "Free coffee with every copy of your far-left newspaper. What do you think?"

"I don't know, they're not selling enough papers?"

"Ha! Oh, come on. I noticed when the music press started doing the same. They give them out for free on the tube and start to introduce more political content. It's free advertising for the globalists. They try to get you to think that popstars are opinionated, but they're told to say these things."

Not many people notice the sound of a helicopter going through the sky at night.

Bex had contented herself to thinking it was just SAS counterterrorism doing routine activity in the area, ruling out the possibility of it being air ambulance, police or military due to the circular pattern of the flight path. And yet there's always the sneaking suspicion that it could be something to do with her.

"Don't you think it's more likely to be crime-related?" says Jarod.

She shakes her head impatiently.

"It's not easy to understand covert harassment tactics if you yourself have never been targeted."

"What are we doing that's so important it would make them want to harass us?"

"You're right," she says unexpectedly. "Could be news choppers. People doing work through the night. Or a stabbing somewhere – you never know. Wait, listen to this bit …" She turns up the volume on the NOFX track they've been listening to on repeat for the past half an hour.

He pauses obediently for the soaring vocals and chord change on "Linoleum". He doesn't particularly like punk music but tolerates how obsessive Bex is about her favourite band.

He isn't content with the explanation that helicopter activity in the night sky is just routine. That's not to say he sides with her, although he does agree that the rate at which people accept the official explanation of things is insane.

"If you're so concerned about being followed around by undercover cops, then why do you constantly broadcast your whereabouts on social media?"

"It's protection," she says immediately. "If people know where I am from my tweets, they know I'm safe. If I don't update my status for a while, questions might start getting asked."

She leans over the keyboard and types something into the search bar.

The avatar she currently has as her profile picture is Chucky, the villain from the *Child's Play* slasher series. She deletes it and uploads a photo taken at the protest from the day before.

Jarod is still trying to understand.

"What's so terrible about spending the night in Parliament Square? That's not going to be enough to warrant them getting the helipads out. We're not that much of a threat to national security."

Bex splits the foil casing on a chocolate biscuit using her index finger and thumb, and gestures half-heartedly towards the clapped-out computer monitor.

"No, but they want us to think we are. It would only take a few minutes to bring up the sky traffic reports on DuckDuckGo, why don't you do that?"

It's the way she's looking. With the weariness of experience and something approaching disdain.

Jarod takes out his NOKIA 3310, about to dial – then hesitates, and throws down the phone.

"Well, I'm not scared of being put on some sort of list, if that's what you mean. Who cares if they're listening? I've got nothing to hide."

Bex smiles, shifting her eyes to the padded phone cover he uses to disrupt the signal.

"Oh, come on Jarod, you're more intelligent than that. They've got hot-micing software, geolocation tools – built right into your device. Do you think they go to all that effort for your safety? Because they *care* about you? They can switch it on and off and hear everything you say. And I sure as shit don't want to make their job easier for them."

The helicopter passes over again. Without breaking eye contact, she continues.

"You're already on their list anyway, sweetheart. Any number dialled from my phone instantly makes you a person of interest."

People with severe mental illness can't be seen to fill out forms too efficiently or take surveys too willingly. A fear of being monitored is one of the most basic tenets of schizophrenia. Bex knows this, and so she gets Trevor at the Citizen's Advice Bureau to do it for her. The trouble she has these days is with sequencing. Tricantamin withdrawal makes her jumpy and short-tempered.

Recently she's been sharing her script with Jarod, who's getting addicted to them without realising.

It satisfies her to see him getting worked up about the helicopters.

"They're probably scanning for marijuana factories in people's attics or something, they have the infrared technology," she says. "People who go to work and enjoy their weekend are not going to notice a particularly busy Friday night sky … Go on, ring that number if you want. Make a Freedom of Information request. Most people would tell you to stop being so paranoid."

"They're not going to tell us what they're really up to, are they?"

"There you are." She smiles approvingly. "Now you're beginning to see what we're up against."

The photos from yesterday's protest have been posted on an alternative news site. Bex is scrolling through them, trying to see if there are any of the banner drop where she'd seen Compost Mckenzie.

There must have been thousands of people on the march that day, and yet they'd bumped into each other at that precise moment.

She'd initially stopped brushing her teeth because of the fluoride. Now her gums were receding, and a nerve root had become infected on the lower left side of her jaw. Heroin is one of the only things that dulls the pain sufficiently.

On the first Tuesday of every month, she picks up her script for Tricantamin and Dwyerbinthol from a chemist near St Pancras Hospital.

These days you had to be careful what you said in front of strangers in waiting rooms. She'd begun to constantly monitor her own reactions to things, subduing the symptoms of her illness to avoid accusations of malingering. It was paramount that nobody saw her behaviour as suspicious, or they could stop her benefit money coming through. Someone with prying ears and a prior knowledge of her mental health condition could get her done for minor public disruption. But staff on Quartz Ward were unlikely to ever pull rank.

Perhaps Jarod had something to do with it. Going out to get Rizlas in the early hours? Yeah, right. He'd noticed the helicopters too but hadn't wanted to mention it – or they'd put his name on a list as well.

Bex smirks to herself. They can make you think a lot of things when they've got a radionics box pointed at your head.

Usherwoods

Usherwoods is one of London's leading occult bookshops.

It routinely runs an ad for front-of-house staff. The more interesting interviews get reported back to head office, where they run a security check on one applicant – a young woman with links to the darkwave industrial goth scene, and occasional involvement with anarchist protest movements.

Sianne Athers is in her second year at university. She knows nothing of two agents installed at the Waterloo campus: Mac Devlin, a surveillance expert with a passing interest in cryptozoology, and a new tutor specialising in queer theory who has recently awarded her a First for an essay on George Bernard Shaw. He invites her out for a jacket potato one afternoon. His name is Sam Renningstall.

Freshers' week, and many misguided goddesses are drunk on the night bus home, falling over bins and ordering food from the Chinese takeout on the corner.

"I was homeless," she tells a commuter as she steps off the number 91. She calls her friend over to look at the gold tooth she's found in the gutter.

"You ladies are looking crisp tonight," says someone from the window of a red Lamborghini.

They sneer at the creeps before joining the back of the queue.

Sianne's wearing a spiral-boned gothic corset and buckle platform boots, while Bex is dressed in her trademark bowler hat and beaten-up old RAF coat.

The tooth is glinting in the orange street light. Sianne turns it over with her toe.

"Has the new recruit been hitting on you then?" she asks.

Bex shakes her head imperiously so that a stray lock of hair falls across her eye.

"Mckenzie? Nah, he's just a colleague. A colleague and a friend."

Bex and Sianne have formed their own intelligence network. They infiltrate student protest movements with the aim of recruiting the genuine anarchists. To be a member, you have to have a psychic superpower masquerading as a mental disorder. Their rival crew are the Anarcho-Queer Pixies (AQP), headed by Himesh Vianney, the self-appointed leader of the fake dissident collective.

Some manufactured punks with tattoos and pork-pie hats have jumped ahead of them in the queue.

"You can virtually smell the chlamydia coming off them," says Bex, who's recently taken to speaking in a Geordie accent. She's good at accents. A lot of us are.

She's pretty drunk and throws something in a plastic packet across the queue so it hits a hipster in the head.

They rap about fit boys at the protest in a desperate attempt to fulfil roles and stereotypes. Donny, Lonny, Tommy and Tad …

As the black and white tiles begin to switch places with the staircase, Bex phases in and out of conversation. She's mainly talking to herself at this point – or, as she likes to call it, 'conversing with spirits'. She holds up a half-empty bottle of cider and summons her servitor, Jarod.

Sianne's always going out with a genius. She goes for boys who are in some way exceptional, rarely exploring her own potential. It had started with her drug dealer in Watford, Paul 'Hand-it-over' Whiteman. She'd then moved on to her maths teacher, Mr Musgrove.

A competent trickster, she reported things at afterparties that no one could quite believe.

"My first boyfriend was a necrophiliac," she once told a room full of sweating cybergoths at an afterparty.

Jarod was different. Mentally fragile, paranoid, interesting. I liked him from the start. Never figured him for a spy.

The severely intelligent conspiracy theorist had a low boredom threshold and a high IQ. He'd been diagnosed with ADHD and put on Tricantamin when he was still at school. Good with computers, he'd become part of an online forum that focused on geopolitical matters and state-funded protest movements.

His formative years were spent reading up on CIA mind-control experiments, until eventually he found his way to Genesis P-orridge and Robert Anton Wilson. It wasn't long before he was attending industrial tech nights in London, experimenting with LSD, and doing a demolition job on virtually every boundary in the book.

He is now executive vice president of the Langton crew and defers on almost every matter to its core founders, Bex Riley and Sianne Athers.

They sit down at one of the circular tables in the dank basement of the Camden Underworld.

Jarod's friend Tad is drunk on cheap lager. The student had attained a certain cult status a few years ago for jumping the gates to Buckingham Palace. He's also rumoured to have crashed his car while checking out a hot girl.

He boasts that he's been arrested eighteen times.

"We're really hitting a nerve in the arm of the state," he says.

Bex smiles, slightly embarrassed for him. No one takes Tad seriously; he sees himself as some sort of outlaw pirate who goes beyond the bounds to get the truth out to the wider public.

He speaks with an overconfidence loaned from cheesy television presenters, a comedy downturn at the end of his cadences, picked up from panellists on comedy game shows for grown-ups.

"Button cameras, Wi-Fi cameras. It's standard to give our vehicles the electronic sweep," he says, taking out a freshly rolled spliff.

She nods wearily, wishing Jarod would arrive with those beers.

"There's no need for surveillance when everyone's a spy."

Only other magicians realise when Bex is speaking in code.

She suggests there are two types of activists. Those with no marketable skills and therefore no economic value in the eyes of polite society; the storytellers, musicians and shamans who explore the origins of behaviour and aim to root out acquired belief systems. And those who have already surrendered to being led by organised movements such as the AQP, the so-called 'professional protestors' who focus on order, control and division. They are typically students or PhDs, trained by podcasts and fuelled by pharmaceuticals, who base their outlook on the opinions of celebrities, popstars and left-wing feminists, accepting the orthodox narrative and only rebelling within the parameters of the causes given to them.

Her crew of iconoclasts and psychics tended to be less predictable. They'd untrained themselves from the script and gone mad and sought for more. But there was another layer operating beneath the initial pathworking. An aspiration, a drive – call it a delusion – that craved a departure from the consensus reality altogether. The trap some fell into was the tendency to surrender to total hedonism. 'No gods, no masters' was the anarchist philosophy, but a rapacious appetite for drugs and alcohol had somehow escaped scrutiny.

"Communism is the only viable future for mankind," says Tad.

Bex and Sianne try not to burst out laughing.

He begins to describe the boring hard-left pamphlet he's just read in a little bit more detail than she needs – so Bex cuts him off mid-sentence.

"I only just got out of hospital," she says. "We've started doing exposure therapy for my OCD."

He seems grateful for the interruption.

"And what does that involve exactly?"

Being a natural magician, Bex has a vivid imagination and is a very powerful manifester, but she tends to aim it at the wrong themes and, like all students of the occult, is prone to bouts of obsession.

She hasn't mentioned the secret police for at least fifteen seconds and it's beginning to get on her nerves. It usually takes her a while to get to know people, and to short-circuit this process, she tests them.

She's created a vocabulary of codes and catchphrases as a way to trick information out of a new recruit, to establish whether or not they are 'in the know' or merely parroting what they've been taught to think. If the conversation reverts back to small talk, she gets bored. If someone is not responding to her test, she bombards them with a rant about spies.

"Never you mind what it involves," she says. "I made some rather interesting contacts when I was on the nut ward, though I since lost his number – the police intercepted our communiqués."

You'd have to be a paranoid schizophrenic to believe the security forces recruit undercover agents to manage the behaviour of social movements. Careerists like Tad were recruited by rote. Employed in secret and tasked to redirect dissent back into the far left by turning apolitical ravers on to cultural Marxism.

She hasn't worked out which agency he works for yet, but she will.

The first and most important aspect of censorship is the ability to silence people in their own minds. The next is controlling what is said out loud. If someone goes off the radar and stops talking, they send in spies.

Tad holds out the bag of Cutters Choice tobacco. Bad move. Most anarchists are never this generous.

She's noticed he doesn't smoke but carries cigarettes and tobacco with him wherever he goes, just in case someone wants to start up a conversation. Dead giveaway.

His choice of drug is ketamine, but he'll occasionally settle for speed. He doesn't seem like a cannabis user, more the sort who likes to completely dissociate.

"We've been infiltrated, of course," he says. "The cops are all over the college – not to mention the hospital. These are typically police dressed as paramedics. A new division or rank of trainee known as PALS that serve as the human camera of mobile and static surveillance."

She smiles to herself darkly, pleased to hear his assumptions are still wildly inaccurate.

McCartney

In the fading light of the outdoor smoking area, Compost Mckenzie searches his pockets looking for the misplaced tobacco. He unzips the rucksack he's got slung over one shoulder and begins rifling through some stuff. Under his breath, she's sure she hears him say the words, "You cunt."

"Do you want one?" Bex asks him, vaguely amused.

"I don't smoke straights," he says, kindly waving away the offer. She places the pack of Chessingtons back in her coat pocket.

"Aah! Found them."

He strides over to the table, confidently yanking out the chair opposite, and starts to build an elegant roll-up.

Compost Mckenzie has shoulder-length blond hair – which he quite obviously bleaches, you can tell by the roots – and looks like he might have Mexican ancestors.

He's on his eighth coffee and keen to make conversation. He speaks through pouting lips and slightly crooked teeth.

"So. How did all this come about?" he says, carefully keeping it vague.

"We've been doing that stuff over at Parliament Square, as well as occupying various vacant properties around central London. You must have read about us in the papers."

"Yeah, you're part of that Langton crew. I went to a few talks when the occupation first started."

"Really? I never saw you there," she says. The sudden note of aggression in her voice slightly throws him off his axis.

"Yeah. They had all these weird rules and codes of how to speak which slightly put me off."

"Consensus decision-making. The Delphi technique. Comes straight out of the Tavistock Institute."

Compost Mckenzie casts his mind back to the wavey 'jazz-hands' he's seen implemented at various student protests over the years. A sense of containment and structure had come as something of a relief to him at the time. Now he considers the possibility that it was a strategy.

"Grassroots protest has all been a setup since the days Don Druitt was operating," she continues. "What do you think it was that killed him?"

Mckenzie considers this.

"The monoxide?"

She laughs, trying to disguise a slight bruise to the ego. Most people just agreed with her, but this one could think for himself – and was therefore a threat.

"Pass me your phone a sec."

She takes the device off him and stuffs it under one of the cushions before he has time to respond.

"They don't record *anyone*, they record *everyone*. But I don't suppose you've heard of the panopticon."

He nods appreciatively, urging her to continue.

She's wearing her trademark bowler hat and has on a long blue duffel coat, even though the central heating's always cranked up to full volume at the hospital. Bex has made everything about her identity a statement against authority. The choice of clothing is baggy, combative. Purple lipstick that seems to say, 'Stay away from me.'

"Nice badge," he says, nodding at the heart-shaped Union Jack on her collar.

"Oh, this is just to ward people off. They immediately assume I'm BNP or something, just because I don't hate my country."

There's a waft of plaque-breath. One of her front teeth looks like it's rotting.

"These days you're not allowed to be proud of anything, especially if you're British."

"Yeah, tell me about it," he says. "They cut my hair for a shoot once. Made me look like Paul McCartney."

Her demeanour changes. It's as though he's said a trigger word.

"Paul McCartney?" she repeats, distancing herself from him suddenly, her eyes going wide and wary.

"Yeah, you know, like with the short fringe and that. Like he had in the sixties." He motions a straight line going across the top of his forehead.

"Don't get me started on Paul McCartney," she says. "You know about the conspiracy theory?"

"What, the one about him being replaced by a double?" He shrugs, as though it's no big deal. "A lot of people know about it. What I don't get is how they could find someone who looked exactly like him *and* play guitar left-handed."

"Eighteen plastic surgeries," she says immediately.

A bolt of tension hits his solar plexus as he realises she's completely serious.

"What would be the motivation?"

"Control of the music industry. McCartney wrote "Can't Buy Me Love", remember? The Beatles were going to start a revolution."

Bex picks some snot from her nose and begins rolling it into beads between her fingers – a habit done ritualistically when in deep concentration.

"The real McCartney died in a car crash, but the hitchhiker he was with survived …"

"And Lennon? Do you think he was killed by an MK Ultra patsy?" says Mckenzie quickly, emboldened by his coffee.

"Oh. So, you know about the mind control?"

She hadn't expected someone from his social standing to be that well versed on misinformation – but then again, the entertainment industry routinely employed government agents dressed as popstars to infiltrate mental hospitals. The McCartney test is one she uses on everyone at first. If they go along with her, she knows they won't be worth recruiting.

"The doorman did it, apparently," says Mckenzie casually. "Mark Chapman was a – what do you call it – false flag. Primed by the security services. I saw a documentary on it."

Bex shakes her head impatiently.

"See, whenever they make a film about something you've got to question where they're taking your eye off the ball."

He looks up at her again, breaking the spell. She searches his face for clues and realises with a sinking sensation that she's lost a bit of the power she used to have over men.

She pulls the bowler hat further down over her head and extracts another cigarette from the pack.

"Gimme a light," she says grumpily.

Tucking a stray bit of blond hair behind his elf-like ear, he hands her the pink zippo lighter.

"So, are you into all that climate change denier stuff and man didn't land on the moon?"

"Oh, the whole climate change thing is a big con. We're being sold a narrative that suits big business. CO_2 is the gas of life. I'm a defender of biodiversity."

"Really, you think it's a psyop?"

"Most definitely. It's more about cloud-seeding and the sun, but it doesn't really bother me 'cos I nearly died of a seizure last year, do you know what I mean? Politics is just a cul-de-sac, another way of keeping us confined to the matrix. It's all a big fun game. I'm a million per cent certain Paul McCartney's dead – but it'll never come out, Ringo's the only one that knows …"

Mckenzie gets up.

"I'm going to the vending machine. Do you want anything?"

"A Lion bar and a Coke."

He turns round quickly and with a cheerful smile says, "You don't think I work for MI5, do you?"

She throws up her hands and laughs.

"I dunno!"

In the toilets, Mckenzie looks at himself in the mirror. He never ceases to be amazed by how good looking he is and wonders why this one hasn't made a move yet. He takes out the wrap hidden inside his shoe and chops out a line of cocaine, sniffs it, and sits down on the toilet. The smell of incense and excrement permeates his stinging nostrils. He flushes, then washes his hands thoroughly.

Back in the smoking room, Bex is sipping her drink from a straw.

"Well, at least we got a Coke out of you," she says darkly.

He's beginning to see what she means by MI5. It isn't supposed to be literal, just part of the mythology she's created for herself. Maybe she just means 'the system'. If you weren't against them, you were for them, complicit. When she spoke in the plural, she meant MI6, foreign intelligence. Yes, that was it – a kind of code. Still on the same polarity, just working for a different aspect. To tune in to her world was to align with a kind of spiritual anarchy. Madness, poetry and Pan. The only trouble was, once you took that decision, it was likely you'd be forever perceived as defective, disordered; a tin-foil hat. It certainly wouldn't do his career any favours.

"I was just joking about the MI5 thing – sorry. I just wanted to see what you'd say," he says.

"And did I pass the test? I mean, as far as I know, I'm not an MK Ultra experiment. But then I wouldn't know, would I? That's the whole point. The term 'conspiracy theorist' is used to discredit anyone who questions the official narrative. Then they can just dismiss you, which makes us easier to divide. Get us to squabble amongst ourselves rather than work together to tackle real issues, not made-up ones like the hoax climate crisis or manufactured terrorism."

"Yeah…" says Mckenzie, who despite his best efforts is beginning to rather like this woman. He decides to mirror her own narrative back to her for a bit – not to flatter, but to show deference. If he makes it clear that he stands alongside her politically, she'll be more likely to invite him to the anarchist HQ to meet other members of the Langton.

"Anyone who talks about one thing too much looks mad," he says. "I mean, we're programmed to think that. Like, when someone's on about an important subject or whatever. I've been mind-controlled to think that to talk about one thing too much is a sign of mental illness. You know … that's how these ideas get dismissed. Why do they call it brainwashed when if anything it's sullied?"

"Now you're talking my language," says Bex. "Put it this way. Six years ago, after one of the sectionings, I found loads of David Icke books at Porchester Library. Now, did someone order them in, or were they put there deliberately?"

"To check who takes them out …?"

"I think they're put there. That way they can see who takes them out and what other books they're getting interested in. If someone orders too many subversive books, they run a security check. They deliberately file things in the wrong section as well, I know that for a fact."

Mckenzie is very interested now. She might be insane.

"Is that how they got to you?"

Bex knows better than to trust drugged-up journalists scouring the backwaters of society for a bit of material. But then again, so far Mckenzie has been able to keep up his end of the conversation.

"I dunno, I'm just a paranoid schizophrenic who lives in a tower block. Don't listen to me. I have fourteen mobile phones."

"Why do you have fourteen mobile phones?"

"I live out near Maidenhead, you know, near the Prime Minister."

He looks at her with puppy-dog eyes. She continues.

"I was writing a book about Princess Diana. Wrote it all on the computers at Porchester Library. They didn't want me working there because I'm famous."

She looks at him out of the corner of her eye, checking for a reaction.

"They're like that, librarians – it's all about hierarchy when you're at that level of the public sector."

She talks at breakneck speed, a globule of white foam gathering in each corner of her mouth. Her accent is affluent, but difficult to discern; a mixture of posh and common, like she's used to melting into what people want her to be.

"I first got tapped up outside Speaker's Corner …"

Braincleaner

Sianne lays there with one eye open, the other half-closed, prodding the new bit of metal in her mouth. A bobble of sebum oozed from the itching wound round the barbell – she could look forward to a nice bit of crust forming there later.

Must have been touching it last night, she thinks to herself. Or could've been the dusty environment. All that dry ice at the Necropolis.

They'd been trying to get to the demo, but Bex had wanted to buy drugs. At some point they'd all gone for a swim in the Lido. Some of the girls had stripped off, but she hadn't.

The public water was a place she might encounter motor oils and fresh bacteria to quicken the breeding of infection in her lip. Interstitial fluids and stagnant microbes. Showers tended to be better than baths, and she broke no rules when it came to oral hygiene.

When she goes to the downstairs room, Jarod is sitting on his own, tapping away on his laptop.

"Were you drunk last night?" she asks.

"Well, I wasn't exactly on the dandelion and burdock. How's your piercing doing?"

She casually opens the fridge and takes out an energy drink.

"It's a bit infected. I can reduce the swelling with frozen ice cubes of chamomile tea," she says, quoting directly from the leaflet that had come with the after-care kit. "But it's not a good idea to drink milk or have too much caffeine if it's newly done."

"It looks skanky."

Usually, she puts up with snarky comments from her boyfriend, but the tiny rod going through her body has imbued her with a sense of assertiveness, an energy transferred to her from the piercer.

"Shut up, I look better than you."

"Wow. Sassy. I like it," says Jarod, who's secretly pleased she got the piercing.

"I'm thinking of getting another one."

"Yeah, cool. You should do what you want."

She shrugs and takes out a mascara wand, applying another layer over yesterday's makeup. Her lips are still stained from the red lipstick she reapplies compulsively, a habit worsened by constant trips to the toilet to snort speed.

He turns to her before she heads out the door.

"I beg you, don't get a tattoo …"

On a slow weekday at ASDA, Jarod surveys the shop floor, keeping an eye out for hot girls and checking his social media profile.

The gay and indie scene tend to cross over at a club called Crave – an all-night bar off Coldharbour Lane.

The bisexual rent boy is already in a relationship but needs to find someone dominant who'll give him a couple of slaps.

Most of the girls he meets aren't that assertive. There is nothing he loves more than the sensation of having his body thrown about and treated like a ragdoll.

He types 'S&M fetish club London' into the search engine and waits for it to load.

He'd first started attending gay techno nights when he was still underage. He liked the sensation of coming up on pills while getting loads of attention dancing on podiums at clubs like Necropolis and Trade. Although he didn't identify as gay, he enjoyed having his arse grabbed and getting dragged off to the toilets. He let men snog him passionately in corridors, and before long was a regular at bars around Soho and Vauxhall.

Dressed in ripped jeans and combat boots, he makes his way to a well-known fetish club near London Bridge. He hears the nasty techno drum 'n bass pumping out of the big brick building on the corner as he approaches. There's a long queue and he wonders if he can jump to the front. Everyone's dressed very fetish, with big platform boots and PVC or rubber outfits. He feels a bit under-dressed, so takes off his shirt, removes his belt, and ties it round his bare chest. He tips a pot of green glitter out into his hands and smears it into his eye-sockets. As he slinks past the queue for the second time, he catches the attention of one of the bouncers, who calls him over instantly.

"You're in," he says, unhooking the rope to the VIP area.

As he steps up into the club, a synthetic humidity hits his nostrils – one he's come to recognise as the potent mixture of dry ice and poppers.

He likes the look of the severe punk girl with a shaved head dancing in a cage by the bar. Jarod isn't a drinker but likes the pills his mate Lee sells for a fiver. Lee tells his punters the ketamine pellets cut with sodium citrate and washing powder are the best MDMA on the market.

"Top-of-the-ladder stuff, this," says Lee, placing the five chunky tablets into the centre of Jarod's sweating palm.

He pops two onto the back of his tongue and washes them down with a vodka and Red Bull.

"Thanks mate, I owe you."

He decides to skin up in the smoking area and wait for someone to approach him – failing that, he can always take to the dance floor until someone crashes into his orbit.

Four hours later, he's stuck in a k-hole sitting on a vinyl-covered rocket launcher. The soaring techno swerves above his head as he slumps weightlessly into the back of a sound monitor, unable to register the loudness of the bass pounding into his skull.

The first time he'd knowingly snorted the glistening ground-up powder had been off a mirror compact in the toilets at the Turquoise Dervish. Since then, he couldn't get enough of the stuff, not realising he'd in fact been addicted to it for years.

He'd built up a tolerance to ketamine pretty quickly, and before long was working as a male escort to supplement his income.

Two red patches below each nostril indicate where he's been inhaling poppers and sniffing the glassy white shards of horse tranquilizer, no longer bothering to smash it up properly using the surface of his debit card.

There have been many drugged-up goddesses that drift through the darkwave industrial goth nights of north-east London. Skin ripped with scars, face young and vandalised by piercings. Sianne had looked the part, but Jarod had a very particular fetish – one that she could not satiate.

The electro-industrial music pushes through his bones and buffers him towards the table where his rucksack is stashed. Inside it is the bottle of vodka he'd snuck in earlier.

"That's goddess," he tells the barman, attempting to point. He tries to unscrew the bottle-top, but his hands fail to obey him.

"Fuck it, I'm having another line." He begins reaching into the bag for the folded-up wrap of cardboard that contains his damp drugs. The barman stops him.

"You'd better not do that in front of me again," he says. "Go to the toilets like anyone else!"

Jarod manages to sober up with a line of speed.

The girl with the shaved head approaches. She stands over him in a PVC bikini, brandishing a bottle of whisky. Immaculate makeup copied from conventional drag queens; face pornographied with drawn-on eyebrows, fake eyelashes and plump, pouting lips. She speaks in animated tones, geared up by speed psychosis.

"Coming to the afterparty?"

"What?"

"Coming to the afterparty? At mine?"

Ketamine and Kundalini

Compost Mckenzie arches his back and reaches for the glass of Genmai-cha tea.

Last night's Kundalini yoga class has woken up his body, unlocking some of the stiffness in his lower spine. Most nights he sleeps in the hammock, as the goose-feather down in his parents' bedroom tends to give him neck-ache.

Today he's got nothing planned except a two-hour therapy session and a swim at the Lansdown.

He tries to locate the Vishnu incense. Funny girl he'd met at the hospital yesterday. Seemed to only want to talk about spies. Said she'd been in a lot of mental hospitals.

He always insists on performing his ablutions before sitting in meditation in front of his sacred altar. He checks the jet of water until it's the right temperature, strips, and steps into the spartan shower enclosure.

His hard body is unusually resilient to extremes of temperature.

After washing and rinsing himself down thoroughly, he emerges from the ginger-and-oud-scented steam, his lower half wrapped in a painfully white bath towel.

A voluptuous array of cushions are stacked in the meditation room, alongside the altar and hammock. Fresh flowers are replaced on a weekly basis by the Filipino housekeeper.

Number 42 Cadrigham Gardens is a classical white stucco dwelling with front doors raised above stone steps in the traditional style – forcing you to look down on whoever enters.

Mckenzie had been a big name in designer tableware since the sixties, specialising in pastry forks, cake slicers and bread separators.

He towels down his body, briefly going up and down the calves and then shimmying across the top of his broad shoulders before thoroughly rubbing down his lower torso, rarely investigating the crack of his own arse. He repeats this action twice, and switches the lights off before leaving, an action done ritualistically, to save on electricity.

Reduce, renew, recycle, that's my motto, he thinks, tipping an ashtray full of cigarette butts into the zodiac crystal wastebin.

He picks up the iPad routinely used for chopping out lines and wipes it down with a silk shirtsleeve.

He can just about make out the dark outline of one new message in his inbox from his agent, Grace, writing to inform him that his band have been taken off the line-up of another UK festival. After the fiasco at last week's recording session, this comes as something of a relief to the young actor, who has been secretly hoping he can leave the band.

My Boyhood in Hell are comprised of models and actors from a leading London agency, and are the creation of music industry executives, with Mckenzie posing as lead vocalist, his image doctored to fit the requirements of the label. He must talk loud, dress like a rockstar and discuss 'controversial' issues such as global warming and war.

A reputable venue near London's Knightsbridge, separated onto six floors, is where he and his agent meet each week.

It's a sweating, overcast day and there are no breadsticks.

Mckenzie sighs and turns to the drinks menu.

The restaurant looks like an airport departure lounge, black wood tables and leather booths. Comfortable. Makes you want to drink a vodka tonic even though you don't usually.

"Why don't you start dating a rapper?"

He slouches in his faded jeans and dockside boaters, shirt untucked, rotating a hunk of raw black tourmaline in his hand.

"I don't really think our interests would be in alignment."

The move to Thayer Holdbrook had gone smoothly, but Grace is disgruntled by the fact that her client has shown so little interest in the new job offer.

"What are you having, a starter?"

He shakes his head and sweeps his unwashed hair under a retro-style baseball cap, unsure whether it's good for him to be associating with someone so shallow and money-driven.

"I'm not really eating at the moment," he explains.

"Can I get you any drinks? Tea, coffee?"

"I hate tea," he muses, glimpsing up at the waiter briefly. "I'll just have a sparkling water and an espresso."

"Latte please, double shot," says Grace.

"You could have anyone," she continues. "Why don't you go for this rapper?"

She brandishes the photo in front of him again. He glances across at the Instagram picture. A white girl with cornrows who looks about sixteen.

"Not my type at all," he says, and thinks back to the girl from the hospital. Infected cheek-piercing. Arms a lattice of scars.

"Yeah, well, she likes you."

"I no longer want to work for the system," he says, throwing down the drinks menu. "With a blog I'll really be hitting a nerve in the arm of the state. It's like John Lennon said, write what you know about."

"Crime?" says his agent, raising a neatly plucked eyebrow.

She crosses her legs and begins to tap away at the screen

of her iPhone XR. She's wearing a semi-fitted tweed field coat with brown elbow patches, and loose-fitting slacks. Under the table she has on DC rainbow skateboard sneakers.

Before joining the agency, she'd been a stripper in Singapore. Born in South London and recruited at twenty-five, she'd initially been taken on by Mckenzie's father to persuade his son away from some of the more undesirable influences at university.

"Why don't you do an article for *Spalding Akad*?"

"Oh, I don't like them, they're pseudo-political. I want to write about real issues. Use my position to make a difference. Maybe I should do citizen's journalism, go for that placement in Kabul."

"They'll take you hostage and kill you."

"Yes, that's true," he admits, somewhat relieved.

The spacious white building, double-glazed, on the corner of the green. Touch-sensitive entry system. Good kitchen and all new appliances. Wouldn't be spending much time there – just a place to crash while you get back on your feet. At least, that's what they'd said it would be like. The other option had seemed much less pedestrian. A psychiatrist's couch in West Hollywood; that stillness that you get in the evenings, the sensation of being walked from a very hot car park into a cool shopping centre. Long afternoons being entertained by stunning shop assistants who were actually all actors.

The only thing you chased was the sensation of relief at the end of a long day, reaching for that finishing line.

It had started in the school playground, that sense of being given freedom. Always chasing the solace of the art block, looking forward to school dinners. The others would be allowed chips 'n' cheese, followed by orange squash and biscuits. But Mckenzie's nannies always insisted on giving him weird packed lunches in stackable tins. Pickled beetroot and other stinky vegetables. Then an afternoon of playing croquet on the lawn. Hiding his balls in the strawberry patch. Craving contrast and chasing a bit of adrenalin, he'd taken the job at Thayer Holdbrook after quitting drama school. But he didn't fit in there either.

His eyes shift to the people sitting comfortably and quietly, chewing with their mouths closed, no music, just the hum of the refrigerators and the occasional screech of fork on plate. No one's getting carried away here, everyone's calm and enjoying the chilled, strip-lit atmosphere.

"It's a cake," says the man to his wife, who's dabbing her forehead with a hanky. He lists the different types of cake. Carrot, lemon, Victoria sponge …

"Victoria sponge," she says, nodding.

There were times in Los Angeles, making things out to be worse than they were. At least he'd improved since then; no more late nights with photographers. Making money just meant saving money, which gave him more anxiety. There were two types of people, really: those who worked, and those who did not. He thinks about the girl from the hospital. Maybe what he needed was to get shouted at by an older woman from a lower social standing. Yes, that rather appealed. No doubt she would give him a hard time.

Something abruptly disturbs his fantasy. A Japanese woman speaking too loudly. The tall man has brought back the Victoria sponge. It's very lonely. Slice.

An orange drink in a glass bottle. She wants ice. He's got a tea, or it could be a coffee. Maybe he needs to be drugged to sit with her.

Mckenzie thinks forward to the next appointment at the clinic and wonders if he will see her again. The girl in the bowler hat.

It's not being work-shy, that's not it. But you get to a point in life where it just gets harder to do things you don't want to.

Everything is down to universal will, and whether you like it or not isn't the point. Self-will had very little say.

The Japanese lady takes out a little hand mirror and does a job of her makeup. The man she's with talks in an overly loud voice to make himself seem more macho. She's drinking a berry smoothie of some kind. Why don't you go back to Japan. Mckenzie's eyes rest on her hands, which look older somehow. Liver spots.

Deep down the big fear, the worry that life will pass you by. Why must she be so aggressive. She has her hair in bunches, bleached strawberry blond, but the roots are showing where she's split the braids at the scalp.

She has made herself up to look up like a doll – and not to be critical, but she just doesn't have a pretty face.

Grace is still talking. He drifts back into her orbit, then out of it again.

"You could move in with Florian, he's looking for someone to rent with in Notting Hill Gate."

Rotting Kill Hate, he thinks with private spite.

Talking very quietly on the hands-free. Makes it even more intrusive. Infuriating to have to be forced to listen. People don't notice. People don't even notice.

"You only need one good version of everything. One hairbrush, Mason Pearson. One good bra, Rigby & Peller, and one bottle of scent. I think you'd suit Spice and Wood by Creed. Bowie used to wear Silver Mountain Water …"

What is she talking about?

He'd finally succumbed to the dreamcatchers. It was tiring to be this observant.

"Here, have some coffee to fuck your sleeping pattern up."

Bex. She'd mentioned the squat she lived in with a bunch of anarchists. Had even hinted that he should go pay her a visit sometime. He could find a number for them easily enough by checking the group's Facebook page.

He concentrates on the space between his wrist and forearm.

He's heard that the tip of a cigarette is hot enough to burn through the nerve endings, which causes more damage and doesn't hurt like cutting does. I'm just doing it for attention, he decides. To claim my body back as my own. Or maybe I just like the look of them. People do things for attention when they need attending to, because they don't feel seen. When all lines of communication fail, you cut out of sheer frustration.

During their last conversation, Mckenzie had been sure to look deeply into the girl's eyes. This tendency to want to seduce everyone he came into contact with had landed him in trouble in the past, and would do so again, just not in the way he expected. Bex Riley was no run-of-the-mill anarchist. She was dark and damned and would curse anyone who tried to save her.

Boarded-up

A boarded-up pub, occupied by ravers, is situated down an alleyway on Hertselt street. It once served as the original Savoy Theatre but had been left derelict for eleven years until the group of anarchists had transformed it into a shelter for the homeless.

A team of vegan chefs work round the clock to arrange a food-run from one of the upstairs function rooms, preparing meals that will be distributed round the streets of London later that evening.

The doorbell doesn't work; visitors are expected to knock loudly and deliver a codeword upon arrival. Mckenzie sends a text to the squat phone before leaving, though in recent weeks Bex has been using it less as part of her protest against the surveillance state.

He remembers her telling him this as he's halfway down the street and throws his head back in exasperation.

He bangs his fist loudly on the door and tries to think of something suitably silly that will pass as a codeword.

"Who's there?" says a muffled voice on the other side of the heavy cobalt insulation.

"Jenny Balstamp – SAS," he says.

After a tetchy wait in the alleyway, there's the sound of a chain being drawn, and a bolt slides the door open. He stands there, grateful but agitated, before Bex, Jarod and few of the others. He notices with an air of regret that the tall girl has tied a tampon to the end of one of her dreadlocks.

"Couldn't hear you, we were jamming."

A warm fug hits his nose as he enters the building. Stuffy as opposed to centrally heated, indicating a basic lack of oxygen. Few windows meant poor air ventilation – making it an excellent breeding ground for moth-eggs.

There's a jangle of bracelets as Bex hits out blindly for the light-switch. A single bar of strip lighting flickers apprehensively, then settles itself on a vast, dark hallway, leading to a flight of stairs.

"This is where you can store the banners," she says.

They follow her into the dimly lit hallway.

Jarod chucks the banners down and stretches his arms.

"Nice rave space. This is even bigger than the one we took on Finchley Road."

She takes a chain of keys from her belt and double locks the front door again from the inside.

"You were there, were you?"

"Yeah, I opened it with Marek the Tooth."

"You 'opened' it? My gosh, how respectable of you."

"Ha, sorry – we're trying not to use the word 'cracked' or 'broke' anymore when referring to … well, breaking into non-residential buildings."

"Are you trying to regenerate the social structure with community spaces or something?" Mckenzie notices the tone of sarcasm she uses when addressing her peers. It's her way of taking power over them. Anyone who's too sincere must be put in their place.

"Hell yeah, something like that. No, seriously, we just want to offer free services to the community."

Jarod turns to Mckenzie.

"We always respect the physical integrity of the buildings we occupy."

Tad Hern has already helped himself to one of the beers they've just got from the off-licence.

"Careful of that cabling over there, some of it's live," says Bex sternly.

"I hear the papers are coming down again tomorrow – that's cool," he says.

Bex never gets asked to do interviews, despite having been around the longest. They'll probably ask one of the younger crowd to do it.

"You got any of that nice spice the Italians always have?" says Tad.

Mckenzie feels concerned at the mention of the lab-sprayed fake cannabis that has been popular on protests in recent weeks. Since being criminalised, it has been pushed onto the black market, where ingredients go unregulated. It is said to cause seizures, severe psychosis, and in the worst cases, death.

"No, last time I smoked that I thought the Simpsons lived next door," says Bex with a nervous laugh.

"I know someone who got heart palpitations so bad they had to go to A&E," agrees a short young man with Sellotape on his spectacles.

"Because spice is cheaper than skunk, it's becoming really popular on the protest circuit, but it's lethal," explains Jarod. "The health benefits and mind-expanding properties of cannabis allow you to see through the programming, which is not what they want."

"Who are 'they'?" asks Mckenzie.

"The globalists."

But Mckenzie isn't satisfied with this answer. Did it mean the one percent, the Illuminati, the dreaded reptilians, or a blend of all three? Of course, no one truly knew. Some said it was all down to influencers run out of Chatham House, the Bilderbergers, Trilateral Commission, Club of Rome and the Council on Foreign Relations.

Jarod wanders into the adjoining room and takes a look round the upper mezzanine. Mckenzie checks out his boxy arse. He's a slender young man with a gothic appearance. Narrow shoulders and muscular arms. Uptight, dignified manner to him. It was easy to see why he worked the pubs round Earl's Court as a rent boy.

"What about those kids in East London getting sent down on some trumped-up burglary charges?" interjects Tad, who always seems to be asking lots of questions.

Mckenzie muses that he could be a corporate spy. Security industry types tended to be rather blatant – unless it was all a cunning double-bluff.

"I don't really know," says Bex, "I've not been around. Got arrested again, didn't I?"

"Oh yeah, for chasing that police car through Parliament Square, that was well funny."

"Yeah, not so funny being locked in a cell for twenty hours and denied writing materials."

The atmosphere changes as they reflect on this.

They continue on up the flight of stairs, now deep into the building.

Tad finally mentions the real reason for his visit.

"So, what's going on with this documentary? Apparently, the film crew have practically moved in."

"Oh, they're all on the AQP payroll. You wouldn't believe how many spies are involved in the protest scene now. It's all the same lot who were doing the fracking, basically. Himesh Vianney, Jill Benion, Foxpiss. You know the names. They say they're activists, but they don't walk the talk. It's just show business."

Bex gulps back the remainder of what's in her can, then pauses on the landing, as though about to be sick. Steadies herself and continues.

"They've never been to this place, put it that way. Jill wouldn't want to get her hands dirty. She's oh so prim and proper. Her brother's a QC."

"Yeah. And?" says Tad.

"And she's an AQP founder. All these agents hijacking the protest to promote their agenda, it's a tactic. They use it to block real, grassroots resistance. With these big, disruptive actions, they bring London to a standstill, and get the bulk of middle England to hate us."

"Which gives the police an excuse to get more heavy-handed and bring in more restrictions," elaborates Jarod. "Eventually, they will shut down our right to protest. You watch. And at the same time, they undermine the actual reason we're here in the first place: to highlight the gap between rich and poor. I mean, this applies to what happened up north with the fracking injunctions. Same groups."

As they go upstairs there's the sound of tinny electronica drifting up from one of the rooms on the first landing. It gets louder as they push open the door.

Mckenzie looks around. A few books are stacked up against a TV, which only plays static.

Sitting on an upturned beer crate, a young man with a shaved head and a septum nose piercing is painting a banner for tomorrow's demonstration. It says: '*Free Julian Assange*'.

"Gonna hold it up at the traffic lights outside the Houses of Parliament," he says proudly.

"This is Dimes. He's not secret police," says Bex, in what will come to be her disconcerting way of introducing certain people to Mckenzie.

Tad goes over formally to shake the boy's hand.

"Pleased to meet you, sir."

Dimes looks up at him suspiciously.

"I don't shake people's hands. And don't call me 'sir'. I don't like the assumed authority the word implies."

Mckenzie grins, enjoying this snotty-nosed teenager.

"Oh, don't mind him," says Bex, thumping the boy on the shoulder. "He's our hacker in residence. Genius, this one. He gets paid to hack computers to test their efficiency. Handy when it comes to accessing the AQP accounts."

Dionysus

The Dionysus is located between a large supermarket on Holloway Road and a Carpetrite. A known 'safe' pub for intelligence gatherers for Bex's private army of anarchist journalists, it also serves as a cheap food outlet for local students at the nearby Metropolitan University.

Framed pictures of Rita Hayworth and Dirk Bogart adorn the entrance hall, harking back to the 1940s when it served as the cinema bar for the nearby Savoy Theatre.

After a day of mixing with student protestors, it's an ideal place for a debrief on the day's events. The huge-ceilinged mezzanine suite leads to a small outdoor area, annexed off from the rest of the pub.

Mckenzie orders himself a Tennessee burger at the bar and sits at the back watching from a table by the smoking area.

Anarcho-queer communist groups like the one run by Himesh Vianney are extremely important to infiltrate.

The NGO activist isn't an anarchist, though he calls himself one. His group are funded by think tanks: organisations that sit above the military, police and government. Their aim is to do away with the concept of the grassroots movement while pretending to be one. They use various covert methods to control the thinking of young, inquisitive minds and ban anyone who questions their guidelines.

Himesh isn't aware of who he works for, and even if he were to be presented with the facts, would probably dismiss them as 'conspiracy theory', a term that he doesn't realise was invented by the Central Intelligence Agency.

His urge to bring down capitalism is a hobby, born of envy and a complete lack of social skills, which has resulted in his distorted worldview. He is now calling for a revolution which he claims will lead to the abolition of private property and free homes for all. He pretty much speaks in slogans and is always quick to mention that he's a practising Buddhist, though no one has ever seen any evidence of this.

It is his belief that his views are his own and that they are the truth, and anyone who disagrees with him requires instant conversion.

Bex said she disliked him in a very general way. He'd once refused her a room at the co-op on the basis of her having mental health issues, yet he went about preaching peace and inclusivity on behalf of minorities. He spends his free time organising protests from his comfy pseudo-squat, condemning the oligarchical structures which his group so closely resembles.

Dressed in a pair of washed-out hareem trousers, a Palestinian *keffiyeh* loosely draped round his neck, he arrives late, pulls out a chair, and takes the earphone wires out of his ears. Mckenzie thinks to himself that these look like microphones used for picking up long-range frequencies. In fact, they are the latest in fashionable iPhone gadgetry, on which he listens to the latest Radiohead album.

His mannerisms include a lot of flapping hands and simpering gestures that seem slightly put on. After a few drinks he tones this down. The two students who arrive early are subservient and seem to be slightly in awe of him. They wait for him to finish speaking, before offering their shy comment.

A tall thin bloke with a punk haircut arrives. His eyes are wide-set and hint towards bisexualism. He leans in at the table with his hands sloping into his lap like a child at a dinner table.

Mckenzie finishes chewing the last few mouthfuls of his burger and wipes his mouth with a tissue. Perhaps it's best to approach the woman first as she seems the most vulnerable.

Before him is a bowl of strawberries soaked in kirsch, a valium and a small bottle of chocolate absinthe.

"That ought to get us through the evening," he says to the girl, winking.

"What working group are you in?" she asks mildly.

"Oh, I don't know."

"I'm doing aromatherapeutic anarchy. Our focus is to find a path through anxiety using essential oils."

Mckenzie's reluctant and already feels bored of these people. Himesh and the others seem to take themselves a bit too seriously. Yoga retreats and meditation weekends. A lot of policing of words, and an obsession with identity politics and labelling. It's like they're trying to rebel by not having a good time.

The ceilings are padded with the thin metal fabric they use in aircraft carriers. Blocks out sting-ray surveillance.

Later that day he'll spark up a Chinese cigarette and recall the encounter to his mentor, Sam Renningstall, who will seem very interested and ask him to gain more of an insight into their holistic approach to warfare.

Redbridge Goths

Another afterparty and the girls are assessing the local talent.

"He's just a poseur," whispers Sianne. "Mixing trad with cyber. Why?"

Bex knocks back some of her cider.

"And what is this ridiculous goatee he's now sporting?"

They're simultaneously fascinated and repulsed by Tad's complete lack of adherence to social codes. He has a habit of mincing and behaving all limp-wristed, as if to give the impression he's a bit gay, in the hope that it will make him more approachable to women.

Sianne suspects he only dresses alternative to get laid and is not really that into the scene.

He takes out a wrap of speed.

"I'll have a line," says Jarod.

"Cool, okay." He looks at the others. "There's no point going to bed for two hours. You may as well stay up and power through or you'll feel like shit in the morning."

Jarod promptly takes out his travelcard and starts rolling it up into a tube shape.

"No, you don't need that, it's base," says Tad.

"Sweet," he says, discarding the curved railcard.

"Here, take it to the toilets. And don't let anyone see or they'll all be wanting some."

The girls watch and sip their cider.

"Where did you get that?" asks Sianne.

"What, the base?" replies Tad innocently. "Bought it off Mad Marek."

"Really?" she says, immediately interested.

Tad has carefully planned all this, playing up his allegiance to the dangerous crowd to impress the girls. It's clear that Sianne likes the psychos.

He eases the big leather coat off his broad shoulders to reveal a surprisingly toned set of forearms. She suddenly gets an image of him pumping away on top of her and recoils in horror at her own mind.

Jarod returns from the toilets looking strange.

"Where's the base?"

"I took it."

Tad's face expresses unprocessed panic which then turns to quiet fury, as he considers the concept of an afterparty without any amphetamines. And the question of what they'll do with Jarod for the next however many hours.

"Jesus, Jarod, you were only meant to dab ..."

The Watford Punks can be heard downstairs causing a stir with raucous laughter and the stereo jammed up. Jarod's discussing why he refused to take part in a recent anti-fascist demo.

"They're just thugs in makeup. They used to beat up goths in Redbridge ..."

He sits upright on the edge of a beanbag, waving a nail-varnished hand dismissively.

"You see, if we resort to violence, they've won. They want you to become violent, because then you've lost control. Those so-called anti-fascist kids are misinformed, they've been led down a cul-de-sac, where their 'rebellion' plays directly into the hands of the state."

"You're just threatened because they'd level you in a fight and you know it," says Sianne.

"That's hardly the point."

"Smashing stuff up is really therapeutic."

"I agree. But do it to a McDonald's or somewhere that deserves it."

At this point, Sianne decides to go down to the kitchen to get another beer.

She's already had half a pill and is feeling plucky and conversational, so she starts talking in an animated way to Mckenzie, who's sitting on the staircase. He wears a plain black T-shirt and a studded leather bracelet on his wrist, and fumbles with the frayed strap of a record bag which is slung over his shoulder. A half-arsed autonomy symbol is childishly drawn on the side in Tippex.

"Saw your post about Hinkley. Are you a bit of a rebel then, Sianne?"

She looks at him blankly. Being on the spectrum, she tends to take everything literally and doesn't understand that he's being playful.

"There are forces supporting us on the Unseen. I'm brushing up on my banishing rituals," she says.

Mckenzie looks her up and down. Her chest is concave, and her body emaciated; her tiny frame almost makes her look pre-pubescent.

He's careful to name-drop bands as it's part of his image, giving the impression that he's into the hardcore and straight-edge punk scene, as well as some of the harder thrash outfits popular with many of the protestors.

He claims to like Fugazi, Flipper and Big Black, but is careful to mention that his favourite band are Pleiadian Vengeance.

They talk for a bit and then go back upstairs.

"That West Ruislip lot are here. The ones who've got the acid," says Bex, with well-timed telepathy. She's been trying to get Mckenzie to drop acid with them as she thinks it will help with his depression. He claims to have been on Tricantamin since the age of fifteen and it's messed with his neural pathways.

"LSD would put you in a better reality tunnel," Bex assures him. But Mckenzie feels reluctant; he's been conditioned by late-night documentaries and horror stories. He recalls snapshots of people with undercuts sitting in bathtubs with their clothes on at his brother's eighteenth birthday party. He doesn't want to end up mad and buying from the reduced section for the rest of his life; years ahead of unemployability, failed credit checks and half-baked conversations about the Illuminati.

"The first time I took it, me and Bex just ended up downloading everything by the Prodigy and listening to it in order," says Sianne.

"That was at the Marylands Road place. I switched on the news and just couldn't stop laughing. It's a bit like going to the Turquoise Dervish for the first time, it changes you."

"Camden changed me," says Jarod.

"For the better," adds Bex.

"I've heard that people who take that path never fully reintegrate back into society," warns Tad.

"Why would you want to? Society's shit. We need to build our own culture." She cocks her head to one side and gives him a funny look. "Theirs is infected."

"You need a complete reversal of ideology. Just say yes," says Bex, and gives him the small dot shaped like a sun on a piece of pink card.

"Acid's a bit 1968. Have a bump of K instead," says Tad.

"No, I don't take that shit."

"Suit yourself. Most of the ecstasy they sell nowadays is cut with ketamine anyway. Here, have a tiny bump, it's not addictive."

He edges a sliver of crushed white powder onto the upturned iPad and gives it to Sianne.

"There," he says, attempting to place it under her nose. With a sudden movement, she slaps it away.

"What part of the word *no* don't you understand?" she shouts.

"Sorry," he says, enjoying the physicality of her refusal.

Time moves slowly that morning. The sun coming up over the Stratford high-rise. Sianne has to leave for the meeting at 10 a.m., as the press are coming to do a feature on the Parliament Square protest.

A lot of people are sleeping or passed out on the floor. She sits in the centre, unable to move or talk.

"Did you take the acid?" asks Tad. He takes out a mirror. Two lines of ketamine are left over.

"Those are for you. Speed," he says, smiling. He knows exactly what he's doing: she won't be able to refuse him in that state.

"You sure? It would really help. I'm meant to be talking to the press this afternoon."

"Yeah, I don't mind if you take all my drugs."

This will make her so incapacitated there will be no chance of her talking to anyone for the next few hours. Meanwhile, he can work the room and find a suitable replacement for the interview.

She snorts the first line, stopping halfway through because of the sharp sting to the inside of her nose, then does the rest using her other nostril.

Tad lights his spliff and gets up.

He's always sure to arrive late to afterparties so that he can take advantage of those who are the most out of it.

Two hours later, Sianne is still sitting there, dribbling and staring ahead; but in her mind she's on the ceiling, in the pipes and the metal workings of the building, inside the song that is playing, inside the fibres of the guitar string, in the third person, melting into the seat beside her, not noticing that Tad is leaning on her leg, stroking the back of her shoulder.

In the toilet everything is sparkling like the inside of a box of soap powder. She's tripping out on the dazzlingly white bath tiles and geometric patterns on the shiny taps. Rows of tiles, all so exact and neatly placed.

She kneels on the floor in front of the toilet and puts the seat down. Tries to unfold another wrap but her limbs are not her own.

She looks into the creases of the folded cardboard. She can't tell if the quantity is a little or a lot, as she's having difficulty with her sense of scale. In one way it does look like a lot; but then again, maybe it's literally only a little speck. Her mind is really tripping out on the sense of proportion, and she can't be bothered to organise another line so just snorts the lot directly off the paper, pushing what's left up her nose.

Everyone is talking about something on the news when she comes downstairs. Her head is still popping and fizzing from the mix of speed and ketamine. She's only had bouncy ket-sleep; her head feels like it's full of candyfloss and her feet seem to have a mind of their own.

She mechanically makes a cup of coffee, but her hands are trembling and she's lost all sense of balance. It feels amazing. She puts the teaspoon of sugar in the milk by accident. No one's seen that, hopefully. She knows that if someone tries to speak to her, she'll either not be able to stop talking or won't be able to begin. Suddenly she feels outraged by the idea of milk, and tips it away, disgusted.

Demo in an hour, she thinks grimly. Got to get back to central. She considers the enormity of the task ahead of her and all the people who'll be waiting to meet her. For some reason, none of this seems very important, and it definitely doesn't seem as important as getting another line.

Her mobile phone is buzzing. She looks down at the popping screen, which is going crazy with letters appearing and then disappearing. She reads a sentence and then sees it split three different ways, the echo of the words repeating and rearranging beside each other inside the screen. Then she thinks everything's about sex.

She manages to make it to the toilet and check her image in the mirror. She's sure two new wrinkles have formed on either side of her mouth, probably from where she's been gurning all night.

She sits on the toilet and cannot seem to feel her bladder to push out the urine. Suddenly she hears a jet of gushing piss and realises it's her own. Afterwards, she pulls up her fishnets and exits the loo, but gets stuck in the mirror en route. Her eyes are big, and she sees how attractive she is. Standing in front of the glass, thinking her hair looks a really good shape.

"You've been standing there for half an hour."

The voice seems disjointed. She turns around to see Bex, eyeing her with a look of disappointed concern.

"What have you taken, Sianne?"

It's impossible. She puts her fingers up to her lips and tries to pluck out a sound. Suddenly, in a very breathless and hurried whisper, she hears herself say something but can't remember what. Time is looping in a two-second memory span.

"Wait here while I get you a drink of water. I told Tad to look after you …"

The group are still downstairs listening to music.

A guy with an ACAB tattoo across his knuckles lifts his head casually.

"They've started the eviction at Parliament Square. It's on the news," he says. "Everyone's gone down to support."

AQP Meeting at the Co-op

A man wearing a dark grey suit gets off the train at Holloway Road, pulling an overnight mini suitcase behind him.

Compost Mckenzie follows him as far as the Carpetrite, then turns left onto the Seven Sisters Road.

It strikes him as odd that the meeting point for a group of anti-capitalists should be above a McDonald's, but having been trained to doubt his intuition, he dismisses the thought, choosing to see it as a symptom of his paranoia rather than a bad omen.

The high street is congested with rough sleepers burning plastic in telephone boxes and making their beds along the dripping bridge.

It's a far cry from the piss artists of Maida Vale, speeding their way across to the local bookies.

Holloway offered severely mentally ill cases. Patients from the nearby Whittington Hospital, dribbling and swaying into the road, launching their bodies at oncoming pedestrians. They spend their days traipsing up and down the bus routes, scouring the ground for cigarette ends, intimidating the locals with ungainly demands for spare change and just generally getting in the way of the Crouch End dream.

Community support officers have been called in to assist with the cleaning up of the area, moving the assorted scum to places where they might be less visible, so as not to sully the view for the locals walking their red setters and spaniels.

A short man with dark, bushy eyebrows has his spot in the doorway to the funeral directors, and sits there fiddling with his rollies, his cans lined up beside him, taking his time to consume the lethal amounts of K-cider. It occurs to Mckenzie on his walk along the W7 bus route that he's seen this man before – he has the same features as someone who regularly attends meetings at SOAS university. One day he'll hear the student activist speak of his homeless twin brother and everything will make sense, but until that day he ponders the concept of the doppelganger, the clone and the simplest explanation – which is that this is an actor playing two parts.

Himesh Vianney had moved to Holloway two years ago, claiming to prefer the socio-economic diversity of a squat to Chiswick High Street. The Anarcho-Queer Pixies meet on a weekly basis to plan their non-violent revolution.

They discuss strategies, tactics and ways of fighting the climate crisis. In addition to this, they wish to eradicate the class system and bring down the patriarchy. They will discuss upcoming court cases, share goals, and take part in what they term 'ice-breaker exercises': rituals in which each member is forced to humiliate themselves by revealing something vulnerable from their past in order to gain trust among the collective.

Himesh had set up the social experiment disguised as a co-op five years ago. He is now the unofficial leader and founder of a community hub for activists, where he functions as a sort of inappropriate father figure to kids half his age.

His Facebook profile describes AQP as 'an anti-capitalist, anti-hierarchical group which aims to fight all forms of oppression'. There are working groups as well as a Compliance Team, who police the attendees by addressing any unconscious bias that might be operating dormant within the group. A consensus-based decision-making technique is implemented to give everyone an equal say. However, in reality, the group has a clear agenda and is run by self-appointed leaders.

Approaching the co-op, Mckenzie stops at the zebra crossing, glimpsing into the windows of the long bendy bus as it slides past him at the traffic lights, its passengers absorbed in their smartphones, no doubt scrolling through censored news feeds, block-booking yoga classes and ordering online from Tesco's 'Freshly clicked' section.

Surveying a row of shops, he registers hunger and scouts for a place to purchase snacks. He doubts the co-op will have any food in the fridge that isn't vegan, and it's a relief to see the bright lights of a newly built independent supermarket across the road. He goes in and buys a net of Babybels, a container of artichoke hearts, some fresh buffalo mozzarella and a scotch egg for later. Walking briskly past the rows of terraced houses on Hertselt Street, he uses his teeth to rip open the packet of mozzarella and squeezes out the water, impatiently demolishing the bolus of white cheese in three mouthfuls.

In his head he rehearses small talk, being mindful of inclusivity, using words such as 'solidarity' and 'diversity'. He decides he'll describe himself as 'gender fluid', rather than straight. Fitting in is vital if he wants to be part of the tribe and align himself to this fashionable subculture of right-minded individuals.

He arrives to find the hallway rammed with bikes. There's a pile of shoes by the door, beneath a mountain of North Face windbreakers.

The sticky lounge is still flickering with Christmas lights

from seven months ago. Half a wall has been spray-painted turquoise, leaving the other half pink.

The stinking toilet bowl is stained ochre, from activists not wanting to flush and waste water.

Stacks of flyers and rolled-up banners clutter the hallway, next to a dismantled children's drum kit and a half-empty bottle of mead. The in-house band have set up their rehearsal space in the main entrance hall.

A ONE LOVE Bob Marley poster takes up most of the back wall, and some fractal fabric prints have been pinned to the toilet door.

A man with My Little Ponies glued to his head in the shape of a mohawk sits on the floor, painting a banner. Mckenzie picks up on the tail-end of a conversation.

"… well, he didn't look like a rapist."

Vianney's keen to ensure a gender balance at the meetings and has rearranged the living room so there won't be any unlevel seating; presumably because being asked to look up at men might be triggering for certain females due to the patriarchy.

In the kitchen, a pot of Turkish coffee simmers on the stove, next to a box of Palestinian imported dates.

It isn't long before people start arriving. Mckenzie finds a place to sit down and takes out his Moleskine and a green fine-point Berol.

Himesh seems disturbed to see some of the anarchists have joined them. He has a strong dislike for the ratty-haired troublemakers who are always looking for a sofa to stay on. Mckenzie feels his heart race when he sees Bex Riley among them.

"You don't mind if a few of us crash here tonight, do you?" she asks.

By the expression on his face, it is clear Himesh would much rather it was only the respectable types from the book group who attended his meetings; however, a peace activist such as himself cannot be seen to turn down a comrade in need.

"No, of course not, it's a solidarity space."

"Cool," she says, evidently disappointed that he's not being more adversarial. "Good to know you're not one of these border police types."

"I'm a no-borders kind of guy …"

The shelves are ceiling-high and crammed with books on imperialism, global warming and non-violent revolution. Mckenzie traces the spines, looking for something interesting to read, and eventually settles on a children's book called *Spot the Dog*.

Himesh passes him a cup of tea.

"Are you taking the minutes?"

"Oh, no. I'm here as an independent. This is my first AQP meeting."

"Welcome, brother," says Himesh, offering him improvised prayer hands and a robotic bow. "Let me give you a word of advice. Don't get involved with that one."

He gestures towards Bex, who's plonked herself cross-legged right in the centre of the circle.

"Why not?" says Mckenzie, squeezing a rooibos tea bag into a cup so that it burns his fingers.

"She's been to prison."

"Oh my God, really?"

Himesh flinches at the excited tone of his voice.

"Yes, and it wasn't a protest-related offence."

"Jesus, how do you know all this?"

"Oh, Bex and I go way back," he admits. "The point is, it wouldn't surprise me if they'd offered her a deal in custody."

"Oh …" says Mckenzie, narrowing his eyes and getting wise to the facts.

Himesh wipes his hands using a Quaker Mission shop tea towel and slings it over one shoulder.

"That's another way the police can infiltrate, by recruiting criminals on the inside and offering them shorter prison sentences."

A tray of polenta cake is brought through to the garden, which is now bustling with an assortment of stereotypes and weirdos. A set of chairs has been arranged in front of a desk and wipe board, and Mckenzie notices an impressive number of mass-produced placards stacked up beside where Vianney is sitting. He wonders where AQP get their funding, as they seem very well supplied for a grassroots organisation.

There's an empty cushion beside Bex, and one next to Himesh. Mckenzie considers it for a moment, then makes a decision that will change the course of his life forever.

"Mind if I sit here?"

Bex offers him a crooked smile through a fraggle of stoned blond hair. "As long as you don't mind me smoking. Didn't think you'd actually show up."

Across from them, Himesh tries to distract himself with pamphlets, his face reddening from the public humiliation of being snubbed. The Mckenzie kid has chosen to ignore his warning, and instead appears to be in cahoots with his rival.

The trust fund activist gets out a book he's been reading, hoping it will impress his new friend. She peeks over at the cover.

"*Behold a Pale Horse*."

"It's really good, you should read it," he says.

"Oh really?"

"Yeah, it's really liberating."

Bex laughs. "And what makes you think I haven't?"

"Oh no, I … I didn't mean—"

"Don't worry," she says. "I'll let you off just this once."

He glows obediently.

The meeting is about to start.

Because of his background in professional protesting, Himesh is used to speaking in front of large groups. He begins with the plenary and then gives a short explanation of his Buddhist practice.

"He's been known to have people forcibly removed for asking questions, you know," whispers Bex. "That's what being disruptive means to these people: being able to think for yourself and question the invisible hierarchy that groups like AQP have in place."

Himesh is surrounded by a captive audience – mostly young students who have read his articles in the press, or seen him speaking on TV, most recently at the well-publicised camp in Parliament Square which AQP have hijacked. It infuriates Bex, who has been around for longer and written a fair few articles herself, all of them self-published.

They begin the meeting. Himesh is assisted by a tall girl in her early thirties with short brown hair and spectacles.

"Who's the chick?"

"That's Jill Benion. Jihadi Jill, I call her. Hasn't been around long."

Jihadi Jill produces a wipe board which contains a list of non-cis pronouns.

"We will first go round and introduce ourselves with our name and our preferred pronoun."

Bex rolls her eyes. "I think I'm going to need a drink to get through this."

"So, I'm Jill, and I identify as 'They'."

Scanning the list of categories on the wipe board, Mckenzie tries to decide which one to pick for himself, knowing full well he'll be less embraced by the meeting if he doesn't comply. Lesbian, Queer, Gay, Bisexual, Bi-curious, Fluid,

Pansexual, Flexisexual, Polysexual, Asexual, Demisexual, TBD, Questioning, Straight …

A few more people take their turn going round. It's nearly his turn. He turns to Bex, who's already started on a beer she brought under her coat. He notices a young man with a gothic appearance cowering in the background.

"Jarod, would you like to introduce yourself?" offers Jill.

"Jarod doesn't believe in gender. Jarod is Queer," says Bex.

There's a warm reception to this, an atmosphere of approval amongst the group.

"And what does Queer mean for you, Jarod?" says Himesh.

Jarod clears his throat, nervous to speak in front of the others.

"It's just about thinking outside the box," he stammers. "The strictures of heteronormativity want to confine us to one state of being. I'm attracted to people, not what they may or may not have between their legs."

He pauses for a second, realising that everyone's still listening. "And so yeah. I just stick to Queer because it's more all-encompassing."

"So, are you gay or bi or what?" says Bex impatiently.

"I'm versatile, you could say. Gender fluid. I denounce the forced role-play of heterosexuality."

She sneers and shakes her head, secretly impressed.

"Sexuality is a spectrum," continues Himesh.

"Yeah, I know that one," says Bex, spitting a few olive pips onto the grass beside her.

"It's more nuanced than people realise. You know, you can be assertive in general life, but still really passive in bed – and vice versa."

"Too much information. Anyway, it doesn't interest me."

She leans into Mckenzie and says quietly, "How does divulging your sexual preferences have anything to do with preventing onshore gas exploration? Or naming the paedos in Parliament?"

She looks at Himesh with thinly veiled disgust.

"How about you Bex, what's your thing?"

Although she has made every effort to decondition her mind as far as possible from the consensus reality, she can recognise the effect she has on this uptight peace activist and knows there's nothing more seductive to a bunch of woke lefties than an abusive bully who won't take no for an answer. Even though she's aware of this, she refuses to play their warped game.

"That's really none of your business."

Himesh inhales deeply and sighs with disappointment.

"One day, Bex, you'll put down your ego for just a second.

"So, welcome to the meeting. I'm Himesh. I identify as 'She/ Her/ He/ Him/They/Them'. As some of you may know, I'm quite active in Nanowore. Our movement has a forty-six-year reputation of achieving change through direct action."

Sitting on what looks like a toadstool, he prevaricates loudly to a captive audience who watch cross-legged, twiddling blades of grass.

It dawns on Mckenzie in this moment that he may in fact be a hypnotist.

"And in all my years of doing this work, what I've discovered is, it is so much more powerful to love your enemy than to condemn him – or her – and to defeat this system of capitalistic greed and patriarchal white male privilege, we need to introduce a new type of anarchy called 'progressive anarchy—"

There's a sudden interruption.

"Well why don't you let a woman facilitate then?"

The room goes quiet because a female voice has spoken. Himesh and many others in AQP already feel a disproportionate amount of guilt over being male, and obediently defer to women wherever possible. At the same time, they feel absolved of responsibility when it comes to other, more obvious issues with their behaviour. It's a case of guilt in all the wrong places. With slightly slurred speech, Bex continues.

"I mean, you're saying you don't want the patriarchy, so then why don't you start here, at this meeting, and have a woman facilitate? I'll do it."

It is at this point that Himesh offers his final shot across the bow.

"I am a woman," he says. There's an awkward pause as Bex momentarily loses her centre of gravity. No one can quite process this absurd and profoundly sinister display of gaslighting.

"But I really like that you made that point, Bex, and my comrade Jill will be taking most of the meeting, just after I've made this last announcement."

"I thought you said you don't identify as a woman!" says Bex, almost losing her cool. "You said you identify as 'They', didn't you?"

"Which is inclusive," says Jill smugly.

"So, this new type of anarchy – known as 'progressive anarchy' – will be one where we aim to help work with the structures already in place, by encouraging the quieter voices to get louder, empowering the working class to make healthier decisions."

"Which isn't patronising at all, is it?"

Himesh shoots Bex a look.

"It would be really helpful if we could have the comments at the end – that way we can involve the whole group."

"See?" says Bex, raising her voice to address the room. "This is how they try and get us back into the system, guys. Train up leaders in Delphi technique facilitation so there's only an illusion of choice. I mean, are we even gonna have any direct-action training today or what? Because I didn't come here to listen to a bunch of reformists tell me that the answer is to vote. I'm here to organise a demo."

Jihadi Jill takes this opportunity to weigh in with her opinion on the matter.

"It wouldn't be advisable to discuss the specifics of an action here, Bex. We will have a portion of the meeting for sharing some of our favourite DAs from over the history of protest in a minute."

"Wait, so you're saying we're not allowed to discuss DA at the DA meeting?"

"On this occasion, we won't be discussing specifics about the action tomorrow due to the very likely possibility that infiltrators may be present at this meeting."

"Yeah, I think they're running it," quips Jarod.

Suddenly there's a commotion in the background. A few in the circle stir uncomfortably.

"I see Tavistock have trained you well, Miss Benion."

Sitting cross-legged, Himesh now patiently turns to face a well-spoken man in an Emporio Armani T-shirt.

"Sometimes having anger is useful, but this is a peaceful protest, and we prefer to deal with things non-aggressively, to mirror the type of world we wish to create."

A lot of grateful nodding then takes place.

This seems to provoke more emotion from the heckler.

"I will reserve my right to speak loudly and aggressively!"

Bex turns to the others.

"That's Gordon Worling, he does a lot of animal rights stuff. He's been off grid for years; I didn't know he was back in action."

"Hypothetical situation," begins Gordon. "A man is holding a knife to a child's throat."

"Here we go ..." says Bex.

"You have a gun. Are you telling me you wouldn't pull the trigger to protect the child's life?"

Himesh smiles and places a hand on top of each of his knees to demonstrate feigned relaxation. He wishes to persuade those observing that he welcomes such questions.

"It's a really interesting point you're making there – and I'm actually grateful you brought it up. Part of how we behave non-violently is to defuse volatile situations non-aggressively. So, we would try another way."

Mckenzie notices he addresses the group inclusively, possibly to escape scrutiny.

Gordon scoffs at this.

"Well, I'd say it's pretty aggressive to allow someone to be murdered in the name of pacifism." He sits back, satisfied that his point has been made.

Emboldened by this truth, another activist now takes their turn to speak up.

"That's not advocating violence though, is it? Think about what he's saying. Why should we accept such sweeping generalisations? I don't want to have their utopia forced on me. I thought this was a democracy. At these protests there's another layer of control operating. They're trying to get us all to speak a certain way so that we think a certain way – and then we just police ourselves."

"Yeah, it's a manufactured movement!" chortles Bex victoriously.

"NGO tripe, AQP are funded by the state!" cries another.

"This is an honourable space," says Jill. "And we have to have boundaries around verbal domination. Bex, you obviously have strong feelings about this, but a few of the people at this meeting have already said they feel unsafe with you being here. Perhaps you'd like to step outside while we address whether or not the group would like to take a vote on it."

"What is that, the progressive anarchy vote with its pre-decided verdict? Leave your meeting? I'd be delighted."

Later that night, Bex is still smiting from the encounter with Himesh Vianney.

"I've read more books than he's had hot dinners," she complains, taking a large swig of lager, causing her heavy bracelets to jangle back and forth and revealing a row of freshly carved scars. Mckenzie notices this but doesn't say anything.

"Social justice warriors make me sick. They want to speak out on behalf of oppressed people with disabilities or from ethnic backgrounds, when they don't even know anyone black or disabled. And then, when someone with an actual disability comes along, they get chucked out!"

"I know," says Mckenzie, who's beginning to realise Bex isn't as mentally ill as she thinks she is.

"It's a fad for most of them," says Jarod. "Something to pass the time before starting on their PhD."

There's a long pause.

"I can't believe you got chucked out simply for expressing an opinion."

"Yeah, Himesh is a journalist though. What do you expect in this day and age? They're all liars and goody-goodies. All on the government payroll. They have no sense of honour or justice."

"Fucking identity politics is bollocks, man. And that go-round thing at the beginning where they asked what pronoun we'd like to be addressed by. All these safer spaces policies, then I get kicked out for having a genuine disability. I mean, what about my safety? I don't feel fucking safe."

Jarod laughs.

"So, erm, change of subject, but what's going on tonight then?"

"I'm taking Bex out," says Mckenzie.

"Why? What have I done?"

"I think he means he wants to take you out … on a date," says Jarod.

"What, and let him buy me coffee in a posh hotel? No thank you."

"Oh, the rejection," sighs Mckenzie coquettishly. "Well, never mind, I'll cope."

She takes a moment to consider this last point, then dismisses the thought and downs her pint in two mouthfuls. Though she's libertarian in public life, in relationships Bex is more like a top-down government. A total despot. She therefore preferred to remain single.

"Thanks for the invite, darling, but there's only one man for me and that's Himesh Vianney. Just because my personality has been stamped and labelled by the state, doesn't mean my ideas aren't worth hearing.

"When all else fails, we must revert to their tactics. Good, old-fashioned coercion."

Later that night, Mckenzie walks out into the cheesy air on Winnet Street. A warm waft of cooked food envelops his nostrils as he turns right at Piccadilly Circus. He hasn't eaten fruit in years, preferring to live off cooked food and Chinese buns. The closest he gets to health is a slap-up meal at the Hare Krishna temple, and even then it's rare.

Bex has informed him that the temple is rigged up to the internal spy network operating out of Friends Meeting House, an MI5 hunting ground.

They put LSD in the pasta, a light sprinkling of lithium in the coconut sauce, and cheesecake laced with MDMA in the cherry icing to keep the punters hooked. If you dare drink a lassi you'll end up on the floor, surrounded by dancing rainbow children clapping their hands in prayer, choking your lungs with incense.

Bex has already urinated twice on the soil surrounding the Jelling Stone at St Katherine's Church, but her bladder is weak. Fertilising a fragile buttercup emerging from the moss, she looks to the sky and contemplates the faces staring down from the pale stone surfaces of the church walls. Smooth wooden doors shut tight against the morning. A spire pointed up into a completely cloudless sky, blue and warm and basic. It had never been her plan to sleep in the park, but she must have passed out at the bus stop.

She has decided to go and face Himesh by herself. Mckenzie's interest in him has bestowed the journalist with a new type of appeal. It isn't friendship she wants. Rather, it has become an unknowable internal drive for control, and to make someone feel as mad and persecuted as she does.

Continental

A continental breakfast on Quartz Ward. Fresh fruit salad and coffees.

"I need parameters," Bex explains to the nurse, sifting out the pips with a metal spoon.

Whole fruits are fine, but berries fill her with anxiety.

Suddenly, she gets an image of herself throwing the plate at the wall. Then decides against it. Best not appear too volatile, she thinks to herself, or they might lock you up for good.

She places the plastic cup beneath the faucet and waits for the tankard to fill with orange squash.

"Unite Against Fascism were a front for the SWP," she tells a dinner lady.

Lunch is always late on a Sunday, as patients are still sleepy from their meds. Bex strides through the canteen holding a plate of waffles.

Pancakes, juice, Marmite on toast, followed by biscuits and coffee.

She's taken the liberty of stashing a few miniature jams in her coat pocket to put in her room later. Odd things like this, done impulsively, help her to look more unwell.

Someone has had a bit of a joke on the wipe board:

Welcome to Quartz Ward +because we care+
T&Cs apply. May be bullshit. Services include:
Proper staff
Unlimited stay
FREE benzodiazepines 24/7
Complementary choice of injections
Regular sedatives
FREE relationship counselling
ALL JUST FOR £499.99 PER NIGHT!!

A television, a row of books and DVDs. Dan Brown. Jeffery Archer.

The painted door with the gold number on the front says 47. No significance to it. Though, on reflection, the 60 milligrams of Tricantamin may have blocked her ability to see double meanings in everything.

In times gone by, she'd have automatically added the numbers together to find their value. 4+7=11. She might then have extrapolated that 11 is the number you get if you add together the letters of the word L-O-N-D-O-N. And London had that particular resonance, a vibration; a spirit so uplifting and electrical that it had recently begun to seem less like a place and more like a person.

She's relieved to be back on Quartz Ward – it's certainly a welcome break from being followed by secret police, having to constantly check if someone's been through her papers.

The visual hallucinations have been on the increase lately, though she daren't tell anyone.

Always play with a few cards close to your chest, that's my advice, she thinks calmly. And recalls the bright grey scales of the bird-like creature that had appeared at the end of her bed that morning, it's large talons and forked tail reminiscent of the dragon at Temple Bar, said to protect the city's hidden treasure.

"I'd like to talk about the incident in Specsavers."

It's 4 p.m. and Bex can't tell if Dr Cruci is an informant working for MI5, or just your everyday mind-controlled spy.

"You said she was an 'MK Ultra optician'?"

Bex cringes to hear her own words repeated back to her. The eye test itself had induced a seizure and paramedics had been called to the scene.

"I've been getting my eyes tested for years. I've never seen a beam that bright."

Then again, your eye health has never been this poor.

"One minute I'm in the opticians. Next thing I know, I'm in the ambulance. They make the prescription too good, so that you have to rely on them more; they don't make money off people that are well."

"Look, I can tell you're quite therapy-literate, so I don't want this to come across as patronising …"

"Please, go ahead," says Bex.

"Forgive me if this sounds rather obvious, but isn't it standard procedure to check the back of one's eye during an eye test?"

Bex nods gratefully for this cool analysis of facts. It may be what she needs. Still, she has to turn the idea over in her mind several times before accepting it.

"The light they shone in my eye is meant to cause damage to the masterclock in the back of my head – the one that regulates circadian rhythms and melatonin production. Sleep cycles."

Cruci shifts in her seat.

"Why would anyone want to do that?"

"I'm afraid I can't tell you that, Dr Cruci."

"Why not?"

Bex notices what might be a tone of genuine curiosity. *Careful, love; your slip's showing.*

"Because it might put you at risk."

As Cruci is talking, Bex thinks idly about the cereal variety packs they have at the canteen, and wonders which one she will choose today.

"The paramedics said you refused to go to the hospital, and that you wouldn't let them take your blood pressure?"

She'd also refused consent to them accessing her medical history, which would reveal a history of mental illness spanning back nearly a decade.

"What can I say? The OCD was just really bad that day."

"How do you mean?"

"It's difficult to put into words."

Bex is smiling slightly but stops herself as soon as she becomes aware of it.

She can no longer smell the BO wafting out from her own armpits. It was a cliché that mentally ill people tended to refrain from washing, but she had to make a special effort. Sitting alone in her room, she'd brought her jeans up to her nose to sniff the crotch – the smell of piss had been invigorating.

"I made my first mistake after the eye test by giving them a made-up address."

"Why did you lie?" asks Dr Cruci.

"I don't know, it was instinctual. I didn't know they were going to go round and check."

"Are you worried if the police have your address?"

"I worry that they went and published it in a leading newspaper."

"Why did they do that? Do you think they were trying to scare you?"

"No, it's to scare the people reading it. The potential activists who might want to support our cause and join in with the protest."

"Do you find being on these protests helpful? I mean, for your mental health?"

Bex wants to mention a call that had come through to her landline a few months ago. Upon answering it, she'd heard a recording of her own voice being played back to her. Around this time, she'd put her name into an internet search engine, and instead of the usual photos of police cordons and demos, had seen one of her and Jarod holding a banner outside the Houses of Parliament. A few photos along, there was now a stark image of two freshly dug graves. It certainly got the message home.

"You seem to be spending an awful lot of time at the protest," says Dr Cruci.

"Yeah …"

"And you often speak of the journalist, Himesh Vianney. In what capacity do you know each other?"

Bex pauses calmly, gathering her thoughts.

"I was a procurer for him."

Years ago, Bex had abandoned domesticity for what she termed 'an interesting life'. It was perilous at times, but certainly an adventure. She much preferred to be nomadic than live in a flat with all the nice appliances. Some that could tune you to unsafe frequencies.

She could have stayed on that well-worn path and done exactly as expected. Been a drug addict in therapy for the rest of her life.

On the night of the eye test, she'd been indoors, drinking as usual, when the doorbell had rung. She was used to friends dropping in, but that evening she wasn't in the mood for seeing anyone. So, when the footsteps had trailed away, she'd gone out to purchase some cigarettes from the local newsagents. That's when they'd sent someone in to rifle through her papers, pour water onto the kitchen counter and throw her duvet out the window.

"I keep dreaming about the car boot sale in Pimlico."

"I didn't know you knew Belgravia."

"The whole area's an MI5 hunting ground. Agents sent as plants to lure out potential targets."

A few years ago, Bex had begun to think certain areas in South London looked unreal, like a set. Actors employed to go undercover on market stalls. This place held a particular fascination for her, due to its grisly proximity to the notorious Dolphin Square building that overlooked the car park.

At first, she'd thought it was a coincidence. The woman selling anti-vaccination T-shirts standing on her own at the back. Generally, agents were trained to gain vital information out of targets in no more than a few sentences. Cigarettes were a good conversation-opener. Before you knew it, they'd told you why they were there, how often they'd been – and perhaps even their postcode.

Of course, they already knew these things. It was just a way for them to determine how willingly you gave away private information.

The Fleeced Lamb

Staff at The Fleeced Lamb are very pleasant. Mckenzie situates himself at the back. By mid-afternoon there's a healthy gathering of local city workers in the upstairs bar.

Leafing through a copy of the *Islington Tribune*, he makes friendly conversation with the locals and waits for the professor to show.

Thirty minutes later, he nervously pushes his way past some of the sweating punters.

"Another gin and tonic please, Andy."

"Your boss not arrived yet?"

He smiles amiably, about to answer – when suddenly an old proverb pops into his head. Loose lips sink ships.

"No, I'm a free agent," he says, smiling.

The figurine in the courtyard had revealed writing scratched into the stone surface close to the mouths of the cherubic fountains: '*Satin's Statue.*'

He'd taken a photograph of it on his mobile phone and now tampers with it in the editing app, changing the filter from sepia to chrome.

Suddenly, he feels aware of someone's eyes on him. In the periphery of his vision, he sees the edge of a white safari fedora. Pasty-faced, full lips, downturned mouth. White hair beneath the hat. The figure of a man in his sixties. Renningstall.

He stares briefly into the dull eyes – and there it is, the slight smile.

"You're late," says Mckenzie.

"Patience is a virtue."

"Yeah, well I hope you're gonna reimburse me for the wasabi peas."

"Anything you need, just ask."

He looks around, a little unsure and scattered. He knows Renningstall is well regarded, has worked at the LSE and King's; and yet Mckenzie always gets the impression he's slightly coercive – it's as though there's a threat behind his words. He isn't sure who or what the source of that threat is but is sure it must be high-level.

"Why do you always insist on meeting me here? I stick out like a sore thumb."

As part of the recruitment process, the secret services carried out extensive research into their assets, usually concluding that a simple overpayment of funds to a bank account would be more persuasive than blackmail. Mckenzie was different. He had too much integrity to ever make it as a spy and was more interested in losing money than making it. In the end it was the guilt he felt over his privileged background that was used as leverage. The fact that he felt it was his responsibility to make a difference, which made him slightly ineffectual, but easy to string along.

"Some of that spice is giving the activists seizures," he says.

Renningstall nods but doesn't say anything. They'd made life difficult for him before and could do so again, if they wanted to.

"It's got to be stopped. A kid smashed up the squat last week after smoking it."

Renningstall smooths his palms together and places them over a green napkin.

"I know, I heard about that. Don't worry, we'll help get it sorted," he says.

Sipping his drink, Mckenzie pulls his beanie hat down over his haircut and gets to the point.

"The core group are close-knit; they've already got a treasurer. It would look weird if I suddenly suggested myself for an admin role."

During their years of research, they'd tried to predict whether Mckenzie would feel any loyalty to the cause he informed on, concluding that he would indeed be the type to turn. And so, they had classed his work as research instead of spying, implying that he was working in the capacity of co-producer for a new TV series.

Unlike those at the protest, he was not middle class; it wasn't going to be a case of him turning traitor.

Renningstall touches the bottle of Perrier to the lip of his glass and pours. He then takes out a long-lens digital camera and begins playing back a bit of the footage from last week's big demo.

"You're right. Someone like Sianne might make more sense. I recommend she be considered for appointment."

Mckenzie's not always sure what the professor's getting at, and something stops him from asking.

The video shows Sianne standing with Bex outside the library. Mckenzie notices that Bex has added green streaks to her hair, leaving the shaved sides blond.

"One of ours?" he says, without knowing why.

Renningstall gives a quiver of his fish-like lip.

"She may be a sex addict, but Sianne definitely knows the magick. She just doesn't know that she knows – and probably best if we keep it that way. It is said that by gazing upon the glyphs in the manuscript, an adept can obtain knowledge of the ancient technology, a science that unlocks a gate in mass consciousness. This knowledge, over time, can reverse the spell on London."

Mckenzie shivers. "Anything cypher-related immediately goes under the Official Secrets Act."

"Yes," admits the professor. "And that's why we change the language: so that it can be achieved by stealth. Sianne's a good-looking girl, and very young."

Mckenzie reflects on the documentary that's being made; it requires another interviewee from the camp.

"Wouldn't it be better to get someone more experienced to talk to the press? I mean, the majority of people getting involved in this thing are just kids – a lot of them are really damaged. They like being at the protest because it's a community for them, a tribe. I don't think it would be ethical for us to use them."

"And I suppose you're referring to Bex Riley?" says Renningstall contemptuously.

"She's different. She's an intellectual," says Mckenzie.

The professor lets out a deep, derisive laugh.

"Oh, come off it. The woman's a complete fool! A dyed-in-the-wool conspiracy theorist. No one takes anything she says seriously. People like Bex lead the movement astray. She's dangerous."

Mckenzie thinks back to his new friend eating a packet of Monster Munch at the non-violent communication workshop.

"Are you sure we're talking about the same person?"

"Believe me, she's got clout. Vianney's more the sort you ought to associate with."

Himesh Vianney's involvement with the cause had made him of interest to the security services several years ago. He'd cut his teeth in the anti-capitalist movement and was now involving himself in more anarchist circles. A person of influence, who also had leadership qualities, was someone they wanted to know.

"Vianney's helping the camp get the right message out to middle England. We're interested in highlighting economic injustice – but putting it in a certain context, you understand. He's worth keeping an eye on due to his work with the homeless. We've been looking into it. State surveillance can only go so far. Whereas if he were to engage in an edgier cause …" Renningstall trails off.

"A lot of them also do hunt-sabbing," says Mckenzie spontaneously. "It's a perfect way to radicalise. We have a place of our own. Some of the others are referring to it as a safe house."

He feels his stomach drop as he realises what he's just revealed.

"Our influence is limited if we remain peaceful," says the professor. "By persuading the group to adopt a more aggressive approach, some real progress could be made. Why don't you invite Vianney to this safe house you speak of?"

Mckenzie has heard Bex and the others argue against the group adopting more heavy-handed tactics. It would mean that a riot would be foreseeable, which could be used by the police as an excuse to shut down the camp.

An ice-cream truck goes by outside, playing the melody to "I'm Popeye the Sailor Man". He thinks back to more innocent times, before his contact with Professor Sam Renningstall.

"You'll never get them to compromise."

"No, I won't. You will," he says, pushing a brown envelope towards him.

He produces a photograph from a file in his padded briefcase and places the laminated sheet on the table. It shows a newspaper clipping of Jarod climbing the gates to 10 Downing Street.

"Pretty boy, eh?" says Mckenzie, with a touch more emotion than intended.

"You will initially make yourself known at the bar where the anarchists go drinking. This is a local pub, next to the Strand campus at King's. It is vital that you don't try to fit in. Jarod is attracted to anti-establishment types. Be loud, talk dirty, and get drunk in public."

"You want me to behave like an old paradigm male?"

Tapping the briefcase, Renningstall unzips the flank and takes out an A4-sized file.

"No, I want you to find out what books he's reading, what music he's into. You could start by looking up the band he's in."

The industrial music scene tended to angle the intellectual knife at some fairly unpleasant themes. Consensual Force, Sinister Minority and Male Teenage Paedophile were just some of the names on the circuit. One of the groups that headline regularly at the Necropolis are Bull Cressida Wick, an outfit led by Jarod Healey.

Healey's willingness to sing about vivisection, communist fascism and child abuse cover-ups has made him a person of interest. His lyrics do not indicate that he agrees with the subjects up for discussion, but his willingness to do so in a manner that isn't entirely black and white has made him a threat to security.

Queuing for one of BCW's shows often results in being shouted at by activists who object to the free expression being exercised, and who mistakenly confuse supporting an issue with the decision to merely discuss it.

Crisis actors are employed to hurl abuse at the so-called paedo-apologists and are sent to listen in on any conversation that may occur in club toilets after gigs.

Anyone who consistently appears at their shows will be put under surveillance for a few weeks, then either dismissed as loons or pronounced mentally unstable 'far-right fascists' by conveniently placed rumour.

Jarod anonymously started a members-only Facebook group in 2022 called The Silver Toilets, but always maintained he was anti-technology. He used it to check the noticeboards for anyone posting about individuals who'd been sent down to investigate him. There was one avatar in particular that caught his interest early on. The username was X29_Taser. Taser initially only posted about the Animal Liberation Front. But animal rights tended to be a gateway cause to lots of other things, including fracking, arms trade and anti-nuclear. Anyone interested in environmental issues would be steered easily using the climate change agenda and given time, pushed back towards employment within an NGO.

However, dedicated animal rights activists were a bit more difficult to control. Especially when they strayed into areas covering false flag events and London's occult symbolism. The aim was ultimately to guide them towards safe subjects, where they could be retrained and put back on track.

The avatar X29_Taser was, of course, Bex Riley.

"From the band's image, it's not difficult to see the singer's a Nazi," says Renningstall.

Having met Jarod a few times, Mckenzie is sure he's not a member of a malevolent paramilitary organisation from the 1930s; merely a fetishist of post-punk fashion – but something tells him not to question.

The afternoon catch-up is nearly at an end.

"Best leave early, so as to avoid that altered state you get into after hanging round the group for too long," the professor advises.

Approaching the entrance to the tube station, Mckenzie notices the outline of a blue-and-white police cordon. There isn't anybody about, not much of a crowd. Just a few police standing round a sleeping bag.

"He's died," says the girl. But the man's hand is still moving.

They take him off on a stretcher and Mckenzie notices someone standing filming it. He looks disapprovingly at the cameraman.

"Well, how else do we stop it?" says the man defensively, as an outreacher tells him to put the device away.

"It was spice, apparently. Quite a few people die from smoking it. It's cheaper than cannabis."

"But how do they get away with it? Isn't it legal?"

"No, it's illegal now – but they get around the law by changing the components."

The rain is coming down as Mckenzie replays the scene over and over again in his mind, wondering if he's seen what he thinks he saw: the man's hand moving. Organ harvesting. A death in the desert. No candles, no tomb. Just a body bag and a twitching limb. A recurring spasm from the spice-seizure, they told him.

On his way home, he drunkenly chucks a beer can into one of the City of London dustbins, observing the emblem on the side. The trademark red and black colours signifying the Magical Guardians of the City's coat of arms.

He's only a few minutes away from the watering-hole where his so-called 'friends' are now drinking, discussing philosophy on the rooftop of the Macadam Building.

It doesn't matter, he thinks to himself. And with a dramatic swoop of his designer duffel coat, he disappears into the warm fug of St Paul's underground station.

Evil Flowers

Two evil flowers in a metal tube. Red tulips, a small device planted into the centre folds of their petals. Upon closer inspection, Bex realises it is a drone.

The canteen on Quartz Ward. Fresh pine disinfectant and clean slate floors.

What can be said of the woman opposite. Her pearls and perfect forehead. Fortunate face framed with tapering fronds of still-blond hair; she did a good job with the dye.

As Dr Cruci talks, Bex listens in a half-trance while her fate is prescribed and decided. Meanwhile, she hears a very low posh accent transmit recordings from a few hours in the future.

References to Porton Down at the junction between Limes Avenue and Brent Street. Spray paint and stickers.

It's strange to think that one day Mckenzie might play a leading part in my stage play, I've never written anything beyond a few Facebook posts.

The low posh accent suddenly increases in volume as the energy of its intention turns towards her, and she awakens and forgets the whole thing.

The pepper shaker was not tapped. Of course, the entertainment industry routinely programmed beggars to think of two-pound coins as benevolent, it was all part of their plan.

She is being called on by the elemental earth-energies, her feet finding their way to an Alcoholics Anonymous meeting.

She fantasizes about her close friend, who she's only just met, the agent known as Compost Mckenzie, heir to an anarchist dynasty and superintendent to a throne of spies.

She plans to move out of the hospital later that day, in exchange for some phone numbers and files.

Suddenly all the staff seem too close. She's closing in on someone tall. Jealousy has gotten the better of the new girl up on Quartz Ward. Her hair's shorter, her spectacles tighter. She adjusts them now to make sense of the Jewess with babe in tum, who froths at the mouth in a dark white cardigan. Thick bejewelled hoop earrings, clasped to her lobe, they are clip-ons.

Six hours 'til take-off, thinks Bex, referring to the clock hanging above the main reception staircase. She handles her papers. Notes seem to correlate with things, points in time. Messages in an old Bic fine point. A recurring theme linked to a CD skipping on a certain lyric. Government-funded radio stations, all 'in the know'. On Quartz Ward they only seem to listen to songs about spies. Well, if you look for it, it's bound to be there. Beware the power of manifestation. That smell, that taste, an overheard sentence uttered too loudly in a hospital café, meant for prying ears.

Tuesday's session reveals very little. She spends most of it remote viewing over different parts of London.

Dipping in and out of conversations, observing unwelcome visitors. An undercover pretending to read the *Islington Tribune* is convinced he's found out the truth about a Euro-sceptic scouting for employment in the fracking industry. He's talking about the prosthetic leg again, sitting there with a pint at the ready. Medication bottles on standby. Close for whatever's coming – maybe a big, long sleep. Or someone called Sabina.

It would be better to leave West Hampstead. The 29 bus, en route back to central. No one detects her Oyster technology, tracking her movements round the city.

She'd formed the Langton crew as a fun alternative to Vianney's controlled opposition. He only wanted people's time and money and to bring to light another meaningless complaint about capitalism, whilst hiding the truth about weather warfare and paedophile rings in Westminster. It hits her like a lightning bolt one afternoon, this need to get back to nature. Away from the soft, swaying evil of a city possessed by wheels; the tarmac-layered panic of Jeep falling arse-over-Porsche.

The sun is out. Windy and solar, with a hint of HAARP. She reads about a tree protest in North Devon and sees herself on another timeline. A better life is only ever a few decisions away. A train ticket will cost too much, but she knows the back routes, the ways to skip the fare.

A few years from now, she'll start going to mediums to make sense of the things she's been seeing. Visions upon waking, crows talking in Scottish accents, rows of cracked parrots. Up close beneath the cloth and straw, he has a pencilled-on mouth and knots instead of eyes.

The train rattles past Victoria. Her eyes are dry, and she wonders if she ought to introduce meat into her diet. She turns up the volume on her Discman – Asian Dub Foundation, "Free Satpal Ram".

Sometimes she sees glitches on carriages, faces repeated on parallel tracks, and thinks she's being followed. But it's just déjà vu, combined with the after-effects of the alcohol.

You want to live out near Surrey, they'd advised her. Everything's faster once you get past Warren Street.

She hops off at Holloway.

The set outside the station is still the same. Stand-in beggars and wannabe junkies begging fifty pence for a battered sausage.

Yeah, they got the paradigm wrong. That's how you can tell they're all actors. Bex smiles to herself, considering the prospect of her odd future. Somewhere a computer wizard is throwing out ideas and letting them settle on stupefied commuters. Albion's army are everywhere. Similar only in the sense that they are all individuals. She will pass through the open barrier at Finsbury Park, then change at Moorgate. There is always a way out.

Victoria Embankment

As she made her way through Victoria Embankment gardens, Sianne wondered if she'd made the right choice by opting for a course in queer theory. Her parents had encouraged a good, solid degree like history or English, and instead she had settled on a module she thought would be subversive.

Increasingly, she can't see the point in what she is being asked to write about. So instead of attending lectures, she has taken to spending more time in the nearby Senate House library, where she sits absorbed for hours in the occult section, reading up on protection magick, animism and conjuring.

The city was a hassle. Buildings had consequences. Baggage checks and rules about using the lift before 5 p.m. Someone with a voice that carries sits a few tables away, talking in animated tones over too much coffee. A play, a theatre production. Was there any point to further education?

An image flashes through her head of walking up and calmly tipping the contents of her coffee cup into the woman's laptop. She imagines watching the uproar whilst remaining completely still.

Everyone had said university would be the best years of her life. A few weeks into her first semester, she'd felt the onset of depression and had been encouraged by a tutor to visit the student support centre. They'd suggested she get some counselling. Three months in, she can already see that talking about it is making things worse.

By the time she was in her first year at university, Sianne had already experienced more hard drinking than most. At fourteen, she'd been sent to a clinic for eating disorders. She only threw up her food occasionally when she'd overeaten or felt sick; it hadn't gotten to the stage where she was an out-and-out bulimic, addicted to the endorphins released post-purge. But they asked such narrow questions in those places, you had to tick every box.

She looks at herself reflected in the mirrors of the downstairs toilets and applies a bit of hairspray to her drawn-on eyebrows to keep them from smudging – a trick learned from some of the older punks at the Necropolis. Bex never bothered to check her look in the mirror, which was one of the things Sianne admired about her.

Before joining the Langton crew, she thought being pretty was the only power she had, and though she is registered with a glamour modelling agency, she is never quite able to accept the totality of her good looks; her eyes often shift to the areas of imperfection she's been trained to notice since adolescence, a habit formed from ritualistically comparing herself to the ads in women's magazines. At twenty-one she can only see the bits in between, the flaws on her face that are the scars of her own judgement.

Two snakebites later, she'll be reciting Reformation poetry and ordering shots at the bar. The antidepressants they've got her on make her incapable of drinking without falling asleep – which is why she has recently started to see the appeal of speed.

There's something about the institutionalised comfort of the student bar that just makes her want to come back and keep studying. One of the few things that brings her any solace is the library, and to keep her membership, she must do the bare minimum of work to stay enrolled.

Before discovering the underground gothic scene, Sianne had worked a number of jobs below her ability level. Retail, boutiques, restaurants, cinemas and art galleries. But the system was getting more rigorous. Small chains were being bought out by larger companies.

It wasn't until she started working at Usherwoods occult bookshop that she'd found anything to really spark her interest. Her name had gone on a list due to a book she had enquired about at Senate House: a manuscript written in cypher which contained an invocation ritual to the Ancient Serpent Gods. She'd only glanced over the text once or twice, not really taking it in; she didn't know this simple act was enough to activate the benevolent dragon realm, which had for some time been waiting to receive the call.

Thirteen statues of dragons surround the City of London, captured and calcified by the dark overlords who controlled the British money supply. The one she is most familiar with is the creature at Temple Bar, who she passes on a daily basis when she crosses the road at lunchtime to get her tuna-melt baguette.

The city is sick. Monuments built on blood; a skyline of spires, old out-godded by new. Some containing the souls of dead children, among other royal secrets. Cover-ups and secret plots. They weren't just statues. These structures were used to house spirits. Wyverns, griffins and serpents had been appropriated by black magicians, turned to dracos and forced to defend the crown. A reversal spell was needed to restore them to their rightful role.

MI5 keep files on individuals who may be considered a threat to security. The combination of magick and her close friendship with the anarchist Bex Riley, a psychic spy obsessed with politics, had resulted in a routine check into Sianne's background.

A red-headed girl wearing a leather coat, who she recognises but can't say from where, orders a small portion of chips. Sianne feels hungry and unwraps the Skinny Blueberry muffin which will take her up to lunchtime, squishing the small morsels between her fingers before consuming the ball of bread. Keeping her weight down is paramount – a desire to be thin is much more powerful than the temporary satisfaction food will bring.

It manifested in little things, coincidences, people showing up in odd places, saying funny things that seemed to suggest something else.

Taking out her notebook, she jots down a few paragraphs highlighted in the main textbook, being careful to stay within the margins.

Revision, she thinks to herself. This is learning, this is what people do. I am very privileged and controlled.

Most of the people at the club last night had been sleazy and mysterious. Where did they go in the day, what were their jobs? Where was Compost Mckenzie at this precise hour?

For no reason whatsoever, she orders a pint of lager.

It was a normal thing to do in the context of being at the student bar, where they seemed to want their clientele to be brainwashed and inebriated. It was equally easy to go shoplifting to get the rest of the books on her syllabus. Why pay?

The student support centre wasn't on the grounds of the main college but situated further along down Gower Street. It seemed rather strange, therefore, that she should end up so easily lost and find herself stood outside the old Port of London Authority building. She liked hanging out there, as the girl on the door was trans and, like her, had an interest in all things occult and magickal.

Inky Blue

A bath towel, covered in inky blue drips, has been draped over the door. There's the far-off sound of a plane going overhead, and the pleasant pitter-patter of early-morning rain as Jarod surveys the empty beer cans and a bottle of hair dye that form the evidence of last night's activities. He closes his eyes again and adjusts to the searing ache in the back of his skull.

That airplane sound, it constantly reminded him of something, but he can't quite pin it to an exact memory. Empty school playgrounds and warm chemists. The smell of toxic detergents and creams for the skin. The brand of hair dye – grade 83. 'Purple Peril.'

He no longer drank for the boozy effect, but more to experience the crushing distraction of being hungover for the next few days.

The old bureau they'd found in the street and hauled up the stairs, now rammed with leaflets and flyers. Hidden in a way that was meant for him to find. Sianne always turned the books that were of interest to her round the other way, so that the spines were facing the wall. A curious trick, intended only to fool herself, they were texts she needed to read but required him to transmit in a condensed way in order to save on time. Sacred symbolism and counter-cultural fiction, written by wizards involved in heterosexual pornography. A fusion of craft and culture that had resulted in an off-colour experiment. Because he has a photographic memory, she gets Jarod to read them for her, then relay the main themes later when she is relaxing.

Lying in bed that morning, he'd hoped to hear her voice outside the window, but she never appeared. It was only a two-month-long relationship, and before that had been about six months of 'courting', which to him meant online stalking.

Alone in her bedroom, he pulls on a purple dress that's draped over one of the beaten-up armchairs and saunters into the kitchen. Popping on the kettle, he takes stock of the room, leaning his skinny frame against the counter.

He makes himself a large coffee using the cafetière. Some posh Compton Street blend. Bex only stole from the best. He then adds two large heaped spoonfuls of white sugar to the mixture.

He looks round the room. No one owns anything at the Langton, everything is shared – however, Sianne has a few things stashed in a suitcase. He decides to go through her stuff.

Leafing through bits of scrunched-up paper and a heap of receipts, he finds leaflets on the Anarchist Federation, stuff about marches against austerity, the Palestinian cause and the obligatory SWP crap. He picks up a pamphlet about the Black Panthers and begins to read. There's a half-smoked spliff in the ashtray, and enough ketamine smeared over the mirror to make a small line. He types the password into her MacBook – which he knows to be 'SabTheCull' – and brings up the latest Ozric Tentacles album on YouTube. She's pasted a small Autonomy sticker over the camera at the top of the screen. 'Good girl…' he says under his breath.

The music collection is all stuff he's recommended. Marc and the Mambas, The Associates, Neutral Milk Hotel, the *Light Work* album by Fliptrix, plus a separate folder dedicated solely to the career of Mogwai. She'd called it his 'dirty stoner music' when they first met. He'd given her points for that. Even though he's submissive in bed, Jarod is the dominant one in the relationship, and ensures this by subtly undermining his girlfriend at every given opportunity. He'd concluded recently that it would be more fun to do this with a girl who was confident to begin with.

It was fortunate that a sense of discipline had been instilled in him early in life, or he'd have totally lost himself in the drugs. He and Bex had tripped together many times and it had welded them in certain dimensions.

He idolises strong women but knows he's too much of a coward to ever go out with one.

A skinny delinquent such as Jarod had to resort to alternative tactics when seducing girls. His looks weren't going to be enough to really cut it with the big boys, but his reputation as a sociopathic pirate outlaw and queer rights campaigner has made him somewhat more appealing – especially to traumatised teens from single-parent families.

After their first encounter, he'd seen what an amazing opportunity Sianne could be. At the time, she'd had a fledgling career in the modelling industry – which would have resulted in her meeting more impressive people. So, he'd implanted the notion in her mind that her image was being sold and repackaged back to the mainstream via a female pop singer called Rayon.

However, Sianne was a sensitive and highly skilled witch, who could channel without knowing it, and was already getting into High Magick. When reading about a subject, she could easily manifest experiments to test her progress. She was already on her path to becoming an adept.

Since working at the bookshop, something had changed. This sudden assertiveness came as a shock to Jarod, who used this as further recourse to pull out the heavy artillery when it came to the gaslighting. He decided to work on her weight, and after that, her career. All the while paying delicate attention to disturbing her sense of reality. But Sianne and her guides could see this sort of trickery a mile off.

Her fascination had really started to take hold. She'd even lopped off her long black hair and started bleaching it bright colours, emulating and adopting Rayon's singing style. Thus, had begun her reversal of the polarity.

He'd encouraged the hero worship at first, claiming it was 'good for her psychic development'.

Perhaps her will was too strong, or on a psychic level she knew what he was up to, but recently every time he tried to get into her head, he'd receive a backlash that simply wasn't worth the effort. Whatever entities were on her case had put up a psychic firewall so strong that even a passing thought in her direction could result in a nasty surprise. Blood in the semen or an inability to get an erection were the first hallmarks of a possession. But the worst was yet to come.

One of Jarod's rules was eighteen cups of tea a day and no pissing. He once stood on a monument outside Parliament Square from 11 a.m. to 11 p.m., never once leaving his perch to urinate. He was known to the team at St Martin's in the Fields, as well as the Camden and Islington services. Registered homeless, or as he put it, 'off the leash'. Getting housed meant being owned ideologically. He earned his money doing a bit of escorting. Sianne didn't mind, in fact she quite liked the idea of her boyfriend being a rent boy – the sleaziness of it appealed to her.

She loved Jarod, and that was why she knew she must destroy him. Or the set of acquired belief systems and conditioned responses that amounted to his personality in any case.

Next door, she listens to him chatting on the phone, putting on the affected voice he uses to speak to some of his older male clients.

She then hears him spray odour-killer through the air, the sound that marks his morning bowel movement. Terrified of his own body, he has to insist on everything being 'decent' by disguising it in toxic chemicals.

It won't be long before his morning purge. He's becoming all the things he hates in her. The myelinated pathways in his brain are now hard-wired to perform ritualistic behaviours pertaining to hygiene and weight.

He'll crouch over the toilet bowl, next to the waste-paper bin full of tampon wrappers and a stolen copy of *The Power of Now*. After barfing up the scrambled eggs and salmon, he'll brush his teeth thoroughly using Colgate Max Strength, rubbing in the stomach bile that will eventually erode the enamel.

Oxygenate

Cordelia Ridge is an eco-village just outside Epsom, built on the grounds of a deserted special needs school. It consists of a couple of bungalows stuck together – what the council refer to as 'blocks' for maths and extra English.

It is one of the last sites where activists can go for respite after weeks of being on the front line. Like most of the occupations round the city, it is being threatened with eviction and is on red alert twenty-four seven.

A place to grow fruit and plant trees, its aim is to stay alcohol and drug-free.

It is said that the occupation has been allowed to go on as long as it has in order to allow the police informants the opportunity to keep the movement under surveillance.

Compost Mckenzie sleeps in the old dyslexia department. Someone has spray-painted the walls red and black and fashioned a curtain out of an *Incredible Hulk* duvet cover. He wakes with his face squashed against the bare mattress, next to an open packet of wafer-thin ham.

At 2.30 p.m., he emerges and makes his way over to the fire pit.

"There's something truly terrible in the shower," he says, kicking a bit of old potato out of his way as he approaches.

"Oh, you've seen it?" says Jarod.

His pallid skin-tone and defeated expression confirm that he has.

"I'd move rooms."

"That's sort of not the point. We need to implement some kind of … border control."

"Build bridges, not walls!" cries Himesh.

"Oh, do shut up," he says wearily.

Himesh looks up and his eyes flash with excitement, as though momentarily enlivened by this adversarial attitude. Checking himself, he reconfigures his mask accordingly and snaps back into role.

"Look, this is a protest site, not a five-star hotel. It was probably just old Paddy. He stayed here after the party. He won't be back – he prefers being on the streets."

"He crapped in our shower – the toilets were right there. That's got to be some sort of statement."

"Look, I hardly think he'd have been together enough to co-ordinate a malicious attack on your toilet. And anyway, it's not your toilet, we share everything at the camp, nothing is owned. He's just a sick old man, he probably didn't even know where he was."

"This is ridiculous."

"Well, what do you want me to do, call the police?"

Mckenzie's about to reply and then stops, remembering that Himesh and Jarod both operate in full-time delusion, firm in the belief that the occupation is a direct cog in the revolution, and that collective guilt is the correct response to all forms of oppression.

It's in moments like this that he finds himself longing for the camp to be cleared and for them all to be evicted, but it's just a passing thought. They decide to go and join the others in the pavilion.

Two security guards pass by on the other side of the fence, near to the open window where the anarchists are keeping watch on the door.

"Good morning," says one of the guards. "Or should I say, afternoon."

Mckenzie has been updating his friends on the shower incident.

"It was deliberate, someone knows about it – they might know about it," he whispers, pointing towards the guards. "I might ask them if they saw anything."

Tad glares at him.

"We don't talk to the scum."

Mckenzie hates blanking people but conversing with cops is frowned upon and it is widely thought that the guards are really secret police employing friendly personas and NLP tactics to achieve a rapport and extract information.

"Got a good fire going in there," says the chatty guard. "Can you cook on it?"

Mckenzie tries hard to save face, then finally caves in under his need for social politeness.

"Yeah, sometimes."

"Probably quite a nice way to live. No job, no responsibilities, sitting round a fire all day having a party. What do you lot do for money, then?"

There's a pause and all that can be heard is the crackling noise of decompressed plastic, as Bex lifts a family-size bottle of cider to her lips.

"I'm not prepared to answer that," says Jarod, pushing Mckenzie to one side, replacing himself as the group's main mouthpiece. "And anyway, what are you talking about? Our entire life is about taking responsibility. For all the wars we've caused, for all the privilege we receive as our birthright here in the British Empire."

"Hmm, interesting," muses the guard. "You planning on staying here long, then?"

Releasing the bottle, Bex gives Jarod the 'I-told-you-so' look.

"I'm probably going to be here … forever, yeah," she says cheerfully.

"Don't you have a job?"

"This is my job."

"Well, fair play to you. I wish I could sit around all day, doing what I felt like."

"I believe you could. Better than working for a criminally corrupt government, isn't it? Wouldn't you rather be out there chasing the real criminals – the paedos and child-killers?"

"We don't get much of a say in it," admits the guard.

"And isn't that a problem for you?" she demands. "They killed Diana."

The others cringe awkwardly, not exactly sure where Bex is going with this. She has recently been off target with her rants and her behaviour seems more erratic than usual.

"What's that got to do with anything?"

"Common ground," she says indignantly. "There are tents in the streets and million-pound apartments left empty. Which we could turn into a community space for one month."

"My wife's into that David Icke," says the guard.

"She's intelligent, then. This country's built on blood. The Crown Council of the Thirteen. Trilateral Commission, Club of Rome, the Council on Foreign Relations – it's not your fucking politicians that run things!"

"Kids nowadays," says Jarod, holding up his hands in a gesture of pretend despair. Bex was like a snorkel to London. A portal to a thousand beers where everything linked back to MI5.

"We know about the military police state and child abuse

cover-ups, those murders at Dolphin Square. I'm calling for the end of MI5!" she cries.

"You know she used to work for IBM?" says Jarod privately to Mckenzie. "Her dad played sax on George Michael's tour of Japan. Now he works the underpass at Marble Arch."

"You seem to know a lot," remarks the guard.

"I worked for the Freemasons when I did catering," she says randomly.

Jarod and Mckenzie exchange glances.

The phone rings, a sample of spooky ghost music.

Bex answers it then hangs up quickly.

"Another hoax phone call from Special Branch. They're trying to trick me into confessing again. Fucking Romanians. Himesh has been taking a backhander at the cop shop, I'm sure of it."

It must be a happy coincidence that so many rescue dogs get named after gods and goddesses of the otherworld. Freya, Zeus and Hercules are being called on for assistance in battle whether their owners know it or not.

On the front line of the Barnet housing struggle, Herc is summoned by a black-bloc anarchist named Carl. The pitbull staffy cross bounds up to his owner, licking the hands of the protestors and scampering past the rows of law enforcement personnel.

Behind the barricade is a locked van containing three caged German Shepherds known by their trainers as 'K9s', bred for their most vicious primitive instincts, to detect drugs, weapons and cash. Trigger, Switch and Target have no place on a demo, but are brought along by the police purely to cause intimidation.

At a fracking encampment in Surrey, Jamie calls upon Artemis, who runs along the edge of a motorway past the site of a new shopping complex, at one time an ancient ceremonial ground for druids.

At Cordelia Ridge, Jarod is ordering Loki to sit and stay. The mongrel is cautious around new people but loves other dogs. He wants to play tug-of-war with a ripped football, but Jarod is talking to Laura, who's come to visit with her seven-month-old puppy.

"He's playful but pretty good with commands," says Jarod. Loki looks up, aware that he's being talked about, feeling his owner's intention through the direction of his voice.

The conversation round the fire is lively. The anarchists are having one of their nightly discussions.

"I don't believe in charities, 'cos they can't criticise the government. CND are independent, which is why they have undercover agents," says Bex.

Himesh listens half-heartedly while gathering up the dried twigs stored beneath his tarpaulin. He shoves them irritably into the centre of the fire.

"Don't do that, you've got to let it oxygenate!" says Jarod.

"Oxygenate?" repeats Bex. "Why don't you just say 'breathe'?"

Jarod shrugs self-consciously and starts rifling through some of the thermal bags.

"Got any soya milk?" he demands.

Himesh finds it difficult to comprehend the rudeness of these people.

"Do you mind asking before you do that?"

Jarod laughs. "I do, actually. There is no 'tea' in proper tea. All property is theft!"

Himesh rolls his eyes.

"You can't just turn up here and start messing the place up. Show some respect."

"Yeah, whatever," says Bex, chucking an empty beer can onto the fire.

"If all NGOs were designed to attract employees, then by that definition, they could not be activists."

Jarod nods aggressively.

"Yeah, completely. If you employ people to do activism then it's not to resist, it's to steer the movement a certain way. Fracking groups have all been taken over by agents to promote the climate change agenda." He looks up to see the reaction this last comment gets.

Himesh patiently lifts the kettle from the fire to pour hot water into each of the mugs. He thinks back to the halcyon days of the nineties road protest when they'd been pushing for the post-structured anarchist society. Housing co-ops and radical routes loan stock, friends running shelters for community interest. There had been real potential then to live without mortgages or banks involved – but that had also been limiting. Soon they let anyone in, regardless of income or ability. Now your garden-variety anarchist would show up – backwater scum whose only ambition in life was to take advantage of the free food and divide the camp by spreading obnoxious conspiracy theories. Unemployable types with a chip on their shoulder that the state 'owed them a living'. Shoplifters and scroungers, mainly – people like Bex, obsessed with the origins of the debt money system, fiat currency and the plight of the many controlling the few. Partly this had become her role in the movement – enlightening others to the corrupt nature of the work–money system. From her accent and bad teeth, he has surmised she is poorly educated and now resents the world for having short-changed her. She openly admits she has no marketable skills but knows how to compel people with language and has most of the young activists in the movement thinking she's some sort of revolutionary.

"Himesh, you need to actually research CO_2" says Jarod. "If you did, you'd realise it's been rebranded as poisonous, when it's not. That way we all get to feel guilty about breathing. See how it works?"

"So, are you two here for the direct-action training?" says Himesh, changing the subject.

Bex scoffs. "I don't need a George-Soros-funded NGO to teach me how to chain myself to a van."

"AQP are funded by the Rothschilds. They're closer to forcing their new utopia on us every day. Gentrification is just the start, it's all part of Agenda 21. People need to wake up." He sips his tea. "This water isn't hot enough."

Himesh quietly thinks ahead to the planning meeting.

Now that the protest is gaining traction, they'll have to tighten security on who they let in. Having had a hand in creating the AQP camp, he's more than a little protective over it; he certainly isn't going to let this sort of low-class scum besmirch its reputation.

Eye Test

In today's session, Dr Cruci wants to return to the subject of Himesh Vianney. Bex is beginning to realise that this theme of the police and MI5 is sounding more like a romantic obsession than a phobia. And therein may lie the key to her whole situation.

"I see him as a character actor in a script for official dissidents," she confesses.

Dr Cruci writes in her notebook that the patient has created a delusion in order to help her cope with life on the streets, concocting an elaborate fantasy that she is a spy to hide the shame she feels about being mentally ill and on benefits.

"Those kids are all cops, programmed by and working for the state," Bex says, referring to her theory about Himesh and his system. "The only way to guide and direct the show is to make the actors believe that their roles are real. You then steer the mindset of the movement, destroying the structures from within, thus freeing yourself from the dreary path of activism."

When she's at home, Bex engages in a pointless ritual. She is in the habit of pouring water on her cigarettes so she cannot smoke them, then, hours later, drying them off on the radiator, lining them up in neat little rows – when it occurs to her that this is a desperate situation, and she cannot quit.

She's due for an eye test. The optician's is a mixture of cream and green, and she can sense from the outset as she steps into the carpeted hall that the lights are too bright for a reason.

It's winter, dark. She's too early. Hunched up, wearing a hat.

Kilburn High Road is busy, and she goes into Sainsbury's to get a few beers.

Later, after the first seizure, she would go back there to find out the name of the woman. They tell her she'd only been there for that day. Bex asks for the name of the device used. The beam had been too bright – a rod going into her eye. Next thing she knows, she's waking up in the ambulance.

Just before she blacks out, she sees her smiling. Dark hair, green and cream optician's clothing.

The paramedics organise her limbs into a seated position. The edges of the ambulance are darkening and smudging in and out of focus. She feels certain she is about to die.

"Go back to Parliament Square," says a voice that sounds like her own but outside of her. Sometimes her thoughts are getting blended in different dimensions. Whatever it wants, it is bound to be located around the Houses of Parliament. Though she has no conscious awareness of what lies beneath the protest site, she is being drawn to return there for magickal purposes.

This knack for shamanism has been with her since childhood. It had often happened upon the brink of sleep, that during the state of hypnagogia, she would be visited by a sense of immensity.

At first, she could not perceive it as a form, only as a sort of pressure all around and above her. Now she realises, with a sensation of pure awe, that it is the dragon on London, the one that lies sleeping beneath Westminster Abbey.

This elemental force was said to protect and guard the city's bohemians, the fragile, the weird, the lost and heretical.

Creatures don't have borders, they fly over fences and crawl under gates, they are not bound by human laws. Once the power of the land is truly tapped into, by the idlers and non-conformists who recognise the old ways, you can form a container to house the spirit.

Two Faces

Bex had two faces. One for sitting indoors with a good spy novel, and one that she snarled through town with.

That day she had on her snarl and went through town with her head bowed down and aimed against the world, marching like a toddler up John Islip Street.

Wearing her navy-blue RAF coat, a roll-up hanging from the side of her thick red lip – some kind of blaze about the mouth, indicating a scrap with the police, or possibly herpes – she glimpses the green and white exterior of the MI6 building, and switches her Paralympics rucksack to the other shoulder.

She'd often contemplated the lewd logo on its side, a crumpled shape forming four letters which blatantly spelled the word 'ZION'.

The far side of the Macadam Building is the beginning point of the demo. A student, showing signs of promise, has scrawled the word 'cunts' under a parking sign outside the side entrance.

Further along, up the Strand, rows of theatres advertise the latest in expensive stage entertainment, as a man in a cardboard box lifts a sign that says, 'Would love a rich wife'. Rough sleepers are not officially allowed to beg on the streets of the city, nor are they permitted to lean against the wall, as it's considered the property of the London Underground.

The student bar is situated in a dank basement outside the main campus. On the opposite wall, a row of large photographs on mounted panels displays numerous graduates from the college, ranging from inventors and authors to poets and diplomats.

Bex had long since given up hope of ever appearing among its ranks; she'd dropped out in her first year at uni and never looked back.

Most of the undercover tramps congregate just round the corner on the doorstep to Millbank Academy, smoking Class A drugs in plain sight of armed riot police.

Darting through the main entrance, she casually clocks a sign pasted to the information board: 'All Students Should Carry Their ID Cards On Them – Security May Ask to See Them at Any Time.'

It's possible she just hadn't seen it there a week ago. Perhaps they'd decided to tighten up on security since then, knowing full well her gang of rabble-rousers will be in attendance at the climate march that week.

The bar is half-empty. "Better The Devil You Know" by Kylie Minogue is playing on the speaker.

She surveys the room, keeping an eye out for Himesh Vianney. He has written another article that week and she has taken it upon herself to visit the blogger in person.

Having checked his social media profile that morning, she knows he will be attending happy hour, before setting off to the march at 1 p.m.

Moments later, she sees him enter the foyer, selecting a table near the entrance to the men's toilets. She watches as he sips his drink and produces a laptop from his satchel.

Posters adorn the walls, advertising the latest election. Sky Television will be broadcasting from the bar that night, the eve of the election result.

An over-fed undergraduate adjusts the feather jutting out of his trilby, and tucks into steak and chips, which look fairly good for canteen food. Beside his hand stands a half-pint of ale. A beige sheepskin coat has been slung over the adjacent chair next to a well-thumbed William Faulkner novel.

It's not long before he places the leather strap of his satchel over one shoulder and walks off in uncomfortable hobnail boots which make him waddle. He's only eaten the meat and left the greens.

Bex gets up, and slides into the empty seat.

In his latest piece, Himesh has described her as an 'agent provocateur', notorious for headbutting fox hunters, and reputed to have been instrumental in the biscuit-tin tunnelling job with Crowbar Jenkins …

She'd been pleased with the article, as it had created more hype around her, and attracted a few helpful animal rights activists to her crew.

Himesh stares into his laptop, pretending to read. When he finally looks up, he is met with the same snaggle-toothed snarl and sad, sparkless eyes of the woman whose name he has been attempting to bring into disrepute for years.

"Hello Himesh."

"You alright?" he says, in a voice tinctured with distrust.

She pulls out a chair.

"No, I'm a bit pissed off, actually."

He gives her a brief glance.

"Is that because you're only drinking a half?"

She smiles, enjoying the mixture of hostility and flirtation that underpins their mock-rivalry. He nudges his plate of chips towards her.

"No thank you. I wouldn't eat any of the food in here anyway – that chef has HIV."

Suddenly she bends over the table and opens her mouth, releasing a mouthful of ale onto the floor.

He observes this with a mixture of fascination and horror.

Wiping her mouth with a raggedy shirtsleeve, she gestures towards the dangly ID card round his neck.

"Any self-respecting human would outright refuse to wear those on the basis that it contains the RFID chip."

"It's odd that you mention wireless surveillance," he says. "I've been writing an article about the global panopticon all week."

"The introduction of ID cards at universities is one of many changes towards government totalitarianism since 7/7. Ever heard of the false flag attacks?"

He shakes his head.

"Seek out my screenplay. It still floats round the web on a Langton fan page somewhere."

"I take it you're here for the protest?" he says, changing the subject.

"Which one?"

"I don't know. Both, I suppose. I didn't know there was a counter-protest."

"Yes, Himesh. An anarchist protest against your government-authorised climate rally. You'd be amazed by how few people are actually checking things like that," she says, hinting at his computer.

"People read my blog," he tells her protectively.

"Same with CCTV. There are so many cameras that no one's looking."

"Oh, I don't know about that."

"Well, I do," she says. "Maybe that's what you should write about – the idea of self-censorship and how it relates to the publishing industry. Writers tailoring their work to fit what they think will sell."

"Which is also a form of censorship."

"Exactly. So, is it written yet?"

"It is. Though I'm half-paranoid that if I publish it, I might start getting followed."

"You don't upload your drafts to your Gmail account, do you? Because that would be a mistake ... Although, better than having someone break into your house at night to steal your papers."

A helicopter goes over the building, purring violently for a second, then swerves off in the direction of the demo.

She anticipates the sea of placards – generic slogans and quoted statistics, in place of real science. She wants to take things further, break up the systems of control, highlight the areas where they are not allowed to question.

She lets Himesh talk for a bit, pretending to be who he thinks she is, and waits to see if he has a personality of his own. Wonders if she will one day see it glinting in the back of his brain, revealing itself under her soft provocation. But the situation is hopeless.

"Today I'm running a media-focus training workshop," he says. "We're teaching activists how to speak about our climate change obligations and get key points across."

Bex yawns rather obviously.

"Who trains your facilitators? AQP are funded by the Rothschilds."

"We receive funding from all kinds of wealthy philanthropists, people who care about the environment and want to make a difference. It's not like all the world leaders are in it together, you know, part of some sort of shady elite."

"No, that sounds about it."

"I refuse to believe it, even if it is true."

Bex laughs at this. Good old Himesh. Talking shit as usual.

"That's okay, Himesh, you're allowed to disagree with me. My opinions are not compulsory."

Getting up, she slings the tattered rucksack over her shoulder before throwing down some dog-eared leaflets.

"I'll see you down at the demo later, after I report back to Chatham House."

Two pints later, she blazes her way through the upstairs bar overlooking the Thames. A low, thumpy piano riff that signifies the opening chords to a classic Madness hit makes her romanticise everything through a filter of beery nostalgia. Some of the students in the booths start bobbing their heads in conciliatory overconfidence, holding up the dregs of their morning shandy as proof that they're not weird without reason.

There's an announcement board in the foyer outside the toilets, and one on every floor of the complicated building with its halls and rivulets. She considers pasting some spoof posters of Dadaist meet-ups and situationist-infused satire. Or introducing some felt-tip pen to the interior of the toilet cubicles. There's already been a feeble attempt written in biro on the door: 'Where's all the art?' it says, next to a sign that reads: 'CCTV IN OPERATION.'

A little bit further down towards Temple, some kids are drinking at a local student union. They have no awareness that the protest they're involved in has been authorised by Scotland Yard.

The spirit of the city sweeps through their thought streams, past the wyvern guardian along Holborn, towards the All Hallows-On-the-Wall in Southwark.

They know not whether these totems are aligned to good or evil forces, and for now, only concern themselves with what they perceive to be a slightly corrupt government situation.

Scuffed

Bex turns the scuffed membership card over in her hand. Black plastic with a silver strip going across the top; it got you in for three pounds less, which was a lot if you were a student. Mckenzie was oh so efficient.

Purchasing membership for the Necropolis was a rite of passage, indicating a degree of commitment, and perhaps dependence on the lifestyle it would inevitably lead to.

She pops the card on the kitchen counter, sliding it back where she found it – beneath his wallet and keys.

The bins haven't been emptied in days. A rich stink has been temporarily masked by someone spraying a can of Lynx through the hallway. She makes a beverage, tea mixed with coffee, and uses a pair of scissors to stir in the sugar; then opens a book she's reading about the SAS.

The covering of the sofa cushion has split apart, revealing a hunk of yellow foam on its underside. It bursts through like an obscene protrusion as she thumbs her way through chapter one: "The Art of Tactical Briefing".

Cradling the mug in both hands, she uses the teabag to swab the edge of the rim – a makeshift disinfectant. It's one of those Cadbury Creme Egg mugs with the graduated beaker shape and thin rim. The milk is slightly rancid, but her senses are numb to the discrepancy. The smell of incense and legal highs fill the air as she sinks into the settee, about to read.

She hasn't had her first mouthful of tea before the peace is disturbed by a gaggle of activists clambering up the stairwell – back from their recent trip to Thames Magistrates' Court. Everyone's been down that day to show support for the arrestees from the DSEI arms fair. Among them can be discerned the dulcet tones of Himesh Vianney. He's been coaching Mckenzie, who was arrested for the first-time last week, on how to conduct himself in court.

"Didn't think we'd be in there that long. They're really dragging it out," says Himesh.

Mckenzie is the man of the moment. Although he can afford one of the top solicitors in London, he has decided to run his own defence.

"It's intentional," says Himesh, taking out a flask and pouring some of the scalding hot coffee into a tiny cap. He sips the dark mixture, relishing this opportunity to inform them all about the British legal system.

"The reason they draw it out for that many hours is to exhaust us. It's part of the punishment – they're trying to put people off doing it again. It won't work. Because instead we make it into a massive publicity event and live-stream the whole thing, and with Mckenzie here, we've attracted the press. This is the best thing that could have happened."

"Oh Mckenzie, you're such a good comrade," says Bex sarcastically. Unfortunately, the lack of emphasis in her voice makes it sound like a completely sincere compliment. Mckenzie turns to her, slightly bashful.

"No, not really. I just did what anyone else would."

"Compost Mckenzie – voice of a generation," she teases.

With a slightly perplexed expression, he turns to address the room.

"So, if anyone wants to do what I did today, feel free to approach me or Himesh after the meeting."

Suddenly a voice pipes up from the back.

"Why don't we plead guilty, though? I don't really get it. Then, surely, we can get back out there and do more actions." It's Marek the Tooth – a new arrival at the Holloway Road HQ who doesn't quite understand the social pecking order of controlled revolutions. He's still full of piss and vinegar, that plucky self-assurance that can easily disrupt the flow of things with the simple audacity to question. He crosses his big arms and frowns at the floor.

"I mean, if we go not guilty then don't we just get stuck in court for ages?"

Himesh turns patiently to Mckenzie as if to say, 'Let me handle this.'

He sizes up the new recruit, a tall man with long black hair in a faded Fields of the Nephilim T-shirt.

"As eco-protectors, we have a moral obligation to uphold the law and save the planet for future generations," he says.

"If we run a necessity defence, we can claim we were acting in the public interest. A longer court case will then ensue, giving us time to build up our campaign and raise awareness."

"Why not get a lawyer?"

Mckenzie turns to him indignantly.

"I don't need a lawyer because I'm not a criminal."

"It's really empowering to stand before the courts on your own terms," says Himesh. "The appearance of the courthouse is designed to intimidate and belittle. The men in black robes hide behind their complicated language, but we know our rights and will not be cowed."

"Hear, hear!" says a girl with a rattail who joined them at King's Cross station.

It's only recently that Mckenzie has been using this new

approach, and due to his status in the group, the others have accepted his views without hesitation.

Himesh continues.

"I was on the front line of the fracking movement. We saw a lot of people lose opportunities by accepting a caution. With the fracking it wasn't just about chemicals leaking into the water due to cracked cement on the casing of the well. It was also about the unforeseen effects. If you are killing future generations through climate change – no matter what the time scale is – it is the job of the court to apply the law."

"Just because it's legal, doesn't make it lawful," says another.

"Fair enough," says Marek the Tooth, who thinks he doesn't know much about all this stuff and really just needs a place to stay tonight.

"The only difficulty here is that climate change is one of the weakest reasons to oppose fracking."

There's a silence as the group slowly consider Bex's statement, then mutually agree to ignore her.

Himesh continues.

"The offence in law is Section 1.2 of the Criminal Damage Act. If you damage the environment in which your neighbour lives, you are doing damage to your neighbour which is intentional."

Bex notices the way he uses his hands to express himself when he speaks, and wonders if he received training at one of the named acting schools associated with the secret services.

"It's not that the climate doesn't change, it does. But that's more to do with solar cycles than CO_2" she says, but the more she attempts to force the issue, the more it seems to confirm something to the others. Not knowing how to respond to her without challenging their own worldview, they silently decide to agree with the consensus – which is that she does, in fact, pose a threat to the overall unity of their campaign.

Parliament Square

Compost Mckenzie is being summoned back to Parliament Square to join a group of thugs who've sabotaged an anti-war demonstration, bringing loud sound systems to blast jungle music and heckle the Quakers who are flying kites for peace. He's been tasked to go down and play the role of mediator, then invite the confused peace activists back for a drink at the safe house with the intention of finding out more about the suspiciously benevolent blogger, Himesh Vianney.

Vianney had struck up an unexpected friendship with Bex Riley when they'd worked at an anti-vivisection stall in Croydon town centre. He'd since attended the occupied site at Hirst Hill, where he was among several activists protesting against the demolition of a local library. Unfortunately, the plan was foiled due to an early eviction, and the team at Special Branch were unable to intercept. He's now a regular at Camp Hamlin, the Langton and Parliament Square protests.

Following research into Vianney, using a database containing lists of his internet browsing history, the Met had brought in someone rebellious and anarchic, with left-wing feminist tendencies. Tad Hern was instructed to arrive late and make inflammatory remarks during an NVDA training, where he would hopefully be noticed by Vianney. His comments about slashing tyres and putting sugar in petrol tanks were intended to rile the blogger, who had until that point been successfully brainwashed by activism. The outcome was entirely successful.

Tad sits on a bench reading a porno mag in the small, gated area in front of Euston station. Eversholt Street is a known hangout for undercover careerists and thieves, subversive bloggers dressed in army surplus gear and scattered medical staff from the nearby UCH.

He's wearing a newish-looking Sea Shepherd hoodie over a purple zip-up fleece and waterproof trousers. A shoplifted coronation chicken sandwich sits untouched by his side, next to a can of supermarket own-brand lager.

He's fairly nonchalant about the various men walking past and decides to go over to Friends Meeting House while he waits to get the call.

A few of the Langton crew sit drinking beer from cans on the pavement opposite Westminster station. They watch with amusement as Mckenzie approaches.

"Hello, Mckenzie. Shit beard," says Bex.

He goes to give Loki a scratch behind the ears, but the dog ducks away.

Bex knocks back some of her drink and stares speculatively.

"So. You've defected to the spy camp."

"Excuse me? What, Himesh? He's alright, isn't he? You don't think he's a spy as well, do you?"

She stares him down, waiting to see how he reacts. Then shrugs and sips her drink.

"I'm not prepared to answer that," she says plainly.

"Look, I know climate change might not be a cause close to your heart, but Himesh has been standing out here for weeks in the cold. There's no way he's a cop."

"Who killed Don Druitt?"

Mckenzie looks slightly winded.

"What's that got to do with it?"

"This was his perch," says Jarod, referring to the relic of pavement where the veteran protestor held his ten-year demonstration. "Megaphones are banned. National Public Order Intelligence Unit, but I don't suppose you've heard of SOCPA."

Mckenzie knows about the new act drafted in to counter free speech; it'd helped the police to drive out leading lights like Druitt who were bringing attention to things the government wanted kept hidden. Its eventual aim being to dictate what activists could and could not protest about.

"So why are they allowed to use one?"

Bex strokes her long pole.

"What I'm saying is, you've got to wonder why some voices are allowed to be heard and others aren't."

He follows her gaze to the gaggle of activists congregating around the tea tent, where Himesh is giving a talk on recycling.

She offers Mckenzie a mug.

"What's in it, coffee?"

"No, cider," she says seriously. It's 10 a.m.

He recalls what Renningstall said about not getting pissed on the job – but it's rude to turn down drink if offered.

He accepts and she seems to soften.

"What did you think of Druitt?" he asks her, reversing the question.

"One of our true cultural heroes," she says. "But these people, they get used. There were legal implications around the alleged obstruction of pavement. What they called 'politically motivated dissent'."

She inhales deeply, then quite out of nowhere hocks up a load of phlegm, spitting it carefully onto the rain-darkened flagstone near his foot.

"Laws brought in to target protestors. And yet that lot over there are allowed to have their little festival – no questions asked. All I'm saying is, it's a lifestyle for them. They're out here because they like being out here. It gives them a purpose. They drafted in that law to counter domestic extremism. Druitt used to use a bell …" she says, tapping her cigarette reflectively.

"Rent-a-mob. Professional protestors," says Jarod, duplicating the description given by Himesh in his most recent article.

"Exactly," says Bex.

Mckenzie suddenly hears himself speaking.

"It's not only about bringing in agitators. They can use other tactics, too."

"Yeah?" she says.

"Yeah," he says shakily. "To discredit someone's reputation, for example …"

She looks him dead in the eye. He sees the haunted hollow look of glazed psychosis. A turquoise blaze about the iris, blasted out from years of Red Bull and Tricantamin. Black bags beneath her eyes, the skin already beginning to look corpse-like.

Suddenly they're interrupted and the spell is broken.

"Hey, it's bowler-hat Bex! I haven't seen you since you got out of prison."

It's Shandy Tomlin. He's come down with some of the Langton crew to support them at the gate. He moves in to give her a hug and a little catch-up session begins. Mckenzie stands around awkwardly. He recognises Shandy from the Langton Facebook page, but they've never met in person.

"Yeah, that all worked out in the end," he tells her.

"The original offence of threatening behaviour was dropped. I called it self-defence – they called it controlled aggression. Doesn't seem fair but ACAB."

"Right, well, that's a result anyway. Can I have a beer?"

"Sure," he says, producing a can of lager from the inside of his duffel coat.

"Hey, there's a party tonight over at the new squat on Charlotte Street."

He looks over at the protestors with ghetto-blasters.

"We've been taking it in turns to rest under the arches where it's still legal to use a sleeping bag," says Jarod.

"And what's the deal with that lot over there? Psyop, correct?"

"Everything's a psyop nowadays," says Bex. "We've just been talking about Don Druitt."

Shandy nods.

"Yeah, we miss Don. He taught us a lot."

"Each night an alarm is set to go off every forty minutes, so someone can swap with whoever's on the vigil. If left unguarded for any length of time, the vigil risks being dismantled by the police."

Mckenzie thinks that sleep deprivation serves as a chilling reminder of torture techniques used in Guantanamo and picks up one of the laminated prints left over from an earlier demo showing detainees in orange jumpsuits sitting in stress positions, their shoulders bowed in defeat. He's already seen the array of candles and placards opposite the gates to the House of Commons.

"That belongs to the London Guantanamo campaign," says Bex, delicately taking the card he has in his hand and placing it back amongst the flowers and tea lights.

"We'll need them tomorrow."

Loki

Never mess with Loki. He might put you in a pub and keep you there for weeks.

Sianne and Jarod have claimed the men's toilets at the new squat on Charlotte Street and are now stickering the walls and writing on the mirrors, spray-painting autonomy symbols and slogans about the police.

Jarod finishes his anti-swastika sign and puts the cap back on his felt-tip pen.

"May as well just put a swastika," says Sianne. "So, how was the meeting?"

"Waste of time. A direct-action meeting where you're not allowed to talk about direct action."

"What?"

"In case there were any undercovers. We weren't allowed to do any planning. All of that has to be done in secret, supposedly, so the meetings are effectively pointless. A perfect way to ensure no DA at the protest on Monday. Nice trick."

"AQP were a setup since day one. Started by the state. This has gone way beyond infiltration. Do you trust him?"

Sianne is staring through a gap in the blinds at Tad, who's sitting talking to Bex in what was once the pub garden.

"Yeah, of course," says Jarod.

"You can never tell, though, anyone could be a spy. That's

why we have to monitor everything on the live stream. It's for our own protection. Seems like a bit of a violation to record people without asking, but what can you do?"

"Oh, they don't mind. Bex thinks everyone's a cop anyway. We live in a surveillance state, remember? There are CCTV cameras on every street corner."

"Yeah, I suppose. I dunno, it just seems a bit daft to provide free footage to the police of our anti-surveillance protest."

"Yeah, I remember when I used to think like you."

"Oh, you patronising cunt!" she says, and chucks a flip-flop at his head.

He ducks out of the way, defending his perfectly backcombed hair.

"And what do you make of Mckenzie?"

"He's pretty much what I expected. I think Bex might have gotten herself permanently banned from the co-op, though."

"Well, people need to be educated," says Jarod. "He's not getting any special treatment just because he's got a profile."

"Yeah, but he was getting worse treatment. Apparently, she was being really hostile."

Jarod refrains from saying anything. His way of indicating that he won't turn on a comrade.

After a while, he offers a vague explanation.

"I think he can take it – after all, she's a woman, so in terms of the power dynamic, he's got the upper hand. And you can't bully someone who's got more economic status than you."

They go quiet for a moment, reflecting on this. Then Jarod adds dismissively, "His uncle's a lord, for fuck's sake – we're the oppressed ones."

Sianne narrows her eyes, peering out through the blinds.

"That's hardly the point. Just because he's a person of peerage, doesn't make what she did okay. Bex was out of order."

"She is the victim, though, Sianne. The mentally ill are one of the most stigmatised minorities in our society."

"Did she really apply online for a job at MI5, or was that just a rumour?"

"Ha ha. Yeah, I think she was too pissed to remember if she actually sent the application. She can speak fluent Mandarin, you know. Used to work for IBM."

"I heard she worked for MTV and went to Oxford. It can't be easy going from that to here," she says, looking round grimly at the spray-painted toilets.

Bex is using a knife to pick the dirt from underneath her nails; a mixture of her own menstrual blood and particles of spliff-sediment. It wasn't that she didn't get the opportunity to take showers, she just chose not to. The feeling of water against her skin was a reminder of how scratchy and uncomfortable her clothes had become. The bobbly texture of an ancient hoodie next to piss-stained underwear just felt worse when the rest of your body was clean. The others blamed the dog, but most of them knew the smell was coming from her. She'd started so many rumours about herself even she didn't know what was true anymore. One year she'd claimed her kids had been taken into care. Said it had been after an ongoing dispute with the neighbours. They'd reported her boyfriend to the police after finding pictures of him wearing a dress on Facebook. Things escalated and she'd pulled a knife on them.

After three months in a secure mental facility, she'd started going to protests to get back at the police – using whatever means was available to her. That had been six years ago.

Sianne closes the window to the outdoor area and pulls down the blinds. She looks round the toilets, bored.

"What should we do?"

"Do you want to wear my clothes and I'll wear your clothes?"

"Sure," says Sianne, who'd suggested the idea to him earlier when he was still asleep. She occasionally took to whispering things in his ear to programme his subconscious mind.

"You look good in a dress," she says, pulling the stretchy fabric up over her chest. She chucks it at him.

"Magenta. I think it's my colour," he says, checking himself out in the mirror.

"Definitely. Matches your yellow eyes."

He shoots her a perplexed expression, then falters, momentarily dumbstruck by how good her body looks.

"That bra looks wicked. You should just wear that to the demo. Put some fishnet tights over it. Punk as fuck."

"Yeah, I think I will."

Jarod goes over to the laptop and skips the first track on *Cleanse, Fold and Manipulate*. He never listens to the lyrics, preferring instead to bask in the image the music gave.

"Can we listen to something else now? We've had this on for ages. It's making me feel aggressive."

"Yeah, that's the idea," he hints.

She rolls her eyes and brings up a Madonna playlist on YouTube.

"You're such a knob," he says affectionately.

She pauses to consider this.

"It's weird how almost every insult in the English language is a derogatory term for the human genitals. Knob, dick, cunt, twat …"

"Pussy."

"Yeah, well that's not really an insult, is it?"

"It shouldn't be. It's meant to associate weakness with girls."

"Hmm. Yeah, I s'pose."

"Gash."

"You don't call someone gash. You can say something is gash. Like, this album is gash."

"Cock, obviously."

"Bell-end …"

She adjusts her bra strap and takes out the pink glitter, squeezing the tube so it blurts out a big dollop, and pats some of it across her eyelids, wiping the excess gel on her tartan leggings. Bex appears in the doorway.

"We're leaving in five. Who's got the Freedom Pass?"

Sianne holds up the small plastic card that ensures them free travel on London's transport system. It belongs to Bex, but they all share it.

They're almost ready for the march. Jarod is militantly anti-nationalism and could get triggered over a patriotic tea cosy. In her gentle but dominant way, Sianne is dealing with this by getting her nails done with Union Jack acrylics, getting him to confront his phobias with her own form of exposure therapy.

"We are responsible for the wars, it's our government that's bombing their countries, I'm not proud to be British, if anything it's shame."

"Yeah," she says, turning up the volume on the music slightly.

"After that demo against the war in 2019," he shouts, "I think a lot of people lost heart."

"Or became more determined."

He opens the door a little more, mascara wand in hand.

"But these days people our age are just into yoga and wellness."

"Himesh is like that. He doesn't drink, apparently."

"I know, it's ridiculous."

"It's a control thing."

Jarod knew about control. He knew how to focus on one thing for too many hours; to push his body to the physical limit.

Before London, he'd slept under stars and woken up on hay bales at various protest camps around the country. Fracking was the cause he stayed close to. Late nights round campfires, relaying tales of FEMA camps and state surveillance. Those were the days when he got arrested every other week for blocking roads and delaying lorries.

Sometime around then, he'd stopped taking the medication. The first seizure had occurred at the Brighton cop shop while loads of people were around him. One minute he was giving a statement, the next he was in the ambulance being carted off to A&E. They ran EEG tests but couldn't find anything.

"His uncle's a QC. People from the owning class are always QCs – Zionists and communists. You can never leave."

Like any addict, Jarod is obsessed with discipline. Sianne understands this implicitly, and, detecting the note of panic in his voice, calls him over.

"Are you nearly ready now? The march will be starting soon."

"Yeah, almost," he says, and steps out. He's wearing a sparkly pink tank-top under a zip-up Adidas jacket, and with his hoodie up looks like a feminine tomboy.

"Let's go …"

Macadam

Himesh is talking to Sianne on the stone steps of the Macadam Building. He's eating a vegan patty and flakes spray everywhere when he speaks. In his hand he holds a copy of *Don't Be Fuelish* by Jenny Balstamp, a famously unreadable hardback. He prevaricates loudly as she politely listens.

"The concept of denial in relation to climate change is what Balstamp rightly describes as a kind of cognitive dissonance."

Sianne tries to look interested, occasionally glancing down at the hairy white toes peeping out from his Birkenstocks.

"What's cognitive dissonance?"

"Don't worry, it's not a stupid question," he says, waving the book so that everyone can see. "This ought to be on the syllabus at every university!" he exclaims. "It's the term used to describe the awkward sensation that comes from holding two opposing concepts in your mind at once."

"Oh right – like being a vegan and buying cat food?"

"Umm. Yeah – that's actually quite a good example."

She tries to dodge another patty-flake as it sprays across the airwaves.

Himesh isn't a threat to the system, but he seems to see himself as one. Sianne habitually plays down her knowledge and vocabulary when in the presence of certain men, and she does not know why.

Many of the more seasoned activists are prone to using complicated analogies that alienate and confuse the listener. Vianney's clever, but not necessarily intelligent. In fact, she thinks he's rather a bore. However, because of his background and demeanour, no one ever seems to challenge him on even the most ridiculous generalisations, and at one point he even refers to himself as black. As he waffles on, she begins tuning in to a conversation going on in the background. A group of new arrivals discussing Tesla-powered electricity.

Himesh seems to sense this.

"I no longer believe in reform," he says suddenly, in a voice loud enough to be overheard by a passing film crew.

Matt Wonger, who runs an independent media outlet based in Bristol, has turned up to interview some of the protestors.

"Mind if we ask you a few questions for our show?" says Wonger.

Sianne looks to Himesh for approval.

"It's probably best if we get a good gender balance in the interviews," he says with a shrug.

She turns excitedly to the film crew.

"Sure, let's do it!"

Matt claps his hands, and they begin to get the cameras ready.

Himesh takes Sianne to one side, out of earshot of Wonger and his crew.

"Remember what we said in the working group. It's about getting those key statements across to the media. Don't mess this up. This is our chance to get the message out to middle England."

"Okay then," she says uncertainly.

Matt Wonger is ready to roll.

"So, tell me why you've come down today?"

In a fleeting moment, she gets a glimpse of herself on another timeline. She'll know something of this incarnation during a future memory of a Kundalini yoga posture – but for now, the narrative of what she's been taught to say runs through her head, versus the rebellious one that starts to bubble up. It's a voice that comes from the intuitive part of her brain, the untapped strand of consciousness that speaks without self-censoring. And though on some level she wants to be accepted, she's tired of sticking to the script and putting out 'key phrases' to the media, which she's memorised but doesn't understand.

Wonger gives her the cue to start talking – but by now her body has gone into protest; she's completely frozen.

"Ummm … errr …" she stammers. "I was against fracking mainly, initially because of it poisoning the water table, and the air pollution. If you think of all those fault lines beneath the earth, it's not wise to drill down so deep. And yeah, as for climate change – I'm not sure. 'Cos you hear a lot of different things, you know? I haven't really had time to research it yet. I know it gets a lot of coverage in the mainstream press – which is controlled by the one percent – so to me that already makes me question it. Whenever I see something like that being given so much media attention, I do start to wonder who's invested in it. I dunno about these big, authorised protests. Like this one today. I mean, are they misdirecting us from some other really important issues? I'm more worried about how we are being allowed to protest about certain things and not others. These people seem really nice and everything, but no one can really answer the questions I have about climate change, no one is willing to do that. They just tell me I'm a conspiracy theorist when I want to debate it …"

"Okay, I can take over from here," says Himesh, grabbing the mic away from her. He turns to the film crew by way of explanation.

"The lifestyle on-site can make some of the activists a bit confused, but essentially we're all singing from the same hymn sheet. We're anarchists, but we want to promote a new type of anarchy called 'progressive anarchy'. This will be a way of bringing environmental issues to the forefront of politics. We support the Seize Party manifesto – they have some really great policies around fracking."

"Speak for your fucking self!" shout a few of the Langton crew who are within earshot.

"Reformist scum! The Seize Party are paedos!"

Himesh smiles nervously, then clears his throat.

"A lot of the kids who've been camped out here for weeks are a bit frazzled. Some bright spark thought it'd be wise to allow alcohol on-site. There's a lot of mental illness in the movement – drinking is their way of coping with the harsh outdoor conditions."

He lowers his voice. "We're not qualified to run shelters for the homeless …"

With an air of derision, the film crew turn back to the girl. But she's already disappeared into the crowd.

A circle of protestors has gathered outside the gates to 10 Downing Street. Placards along the gate display an array of unusual dissent. Tesla Badgers Against Fracking, End MI5, Bilderberg Stole My Hamster …

Jarod photographs the best of them as two police officers from the Tactical Aid Unit, or Tactical Assault Unit, as they're known, slide by in a meat truck.

It's 11 a.m and Bex is already on her first beer. Eyes puffy and bloodshot, dirt underneath her nails, she sways back and forth, a reaction to the cold or perhaps the effects of mixing booze, brown and benz. Friendliness is not her style, but she's secretly pleased to see that Compost Mckenzie has joined them.

"Where's Himesh?" he asks.

She points to the entrance of Westminster station.

"Talking to the scum."

"They're human beings as well, you know," he says.

"We're all a bit shaken," she confides. "Last week Nutmeg was arrested and detained under the Mental Health Act for swearing in front of a TAU."

"Fuck …" says Mckenzie.

It's a tactic that's been carried out by Greater Manchester Police at fracking protests, but the first time it's been deployed at a London demo.

Typically, arrestees will be held in the cells for twenty-four hours and bailed from the area. But the Met have started targeting individuals. Anyone who has been at the camp for longer than a month is being made an example of.

"They don't want experienced activists influencing the newcomers," she explains. "They cuffed me in the van once and threatened to rip out my piercings. Look out for that one over there with the shit tattoos, he's a real psycho. You can see how much he enjoys applying pressure points to teenage boys and getting them in a headlock. Sicko."

It isn't long before Himesh approaches, accompanied by a black-bloc anarchist.

"Well, we're just about done over there. Toby has been helping with the legal support."

"We've met before," says Jarod, giving Toby a reluctant nod.

"Enchanté."

"Don't I know you from somewhere?" asks Mckenzie.

"Perhaps Redwatch."

"Oh, so you're on there as well, are you?"

"We all are. Anyone who stands up against the corporatocracy risks getting their name put on a list."

"Yeah, well, you must know Bill Thompson then."

"I'm no friend of Bill Thompson. He gives names to the EDL."

Mckenzie reflects on this. He's sure he remembers a Thompson from Cordelia Ridge. Nice guy, as he recalls. Gave him a hand building a compost loo once. He decides to keep this anecdote to himself for the time being.

"Okay, let's get on with this," says Himesh, holding up a wipe board and plastic container of olives.

"We were just talking to those police liaison officers over there. Some of them are alright, you know."

"Yeah, it's their job to make you think that: they're intelligence gatherers," says Bex wearily.

"No, I'm serious. That one guy is actually decent. He started telling me he's against foxhunting and everything."

The six-year war between Bex and Himesh had been described as rivalry, but it was deeper than that. Himesh knew what buttons to push, and that it sent her towards an invisible edge. Bex had to be careful at all times, as another protest-related arrest could have serious ramifications for her. Nevertheless, Himesh continued with his game, trying to gently provoke, in the hope that she might get arrested and bailed from the camp.

It's still not clear why they've all come down here. The march has been well attended and they've succeeded in their aim of distributing leaflets. Toby is keen to tell them all about the march against the EDL last week in Brighton.

"One of the fash got cornered on his own – we gave him a right good kicking," he says gloatingly.

Jarod and Bex exchange glances. Without knowing why, Mckenzie suddenly pipes up.

"I'd like to come on an anti-fash march with you sometime. Get out some of my aggression on the racist bastards."

This seems to take Toby by surprise, and he's suddenly looking shifty and uncomfortable.

"Well, you have to know people," he warns. "It's not a good idea for you to go on your own." He looks Mckenzie up and down. "Do you wear contact lenses?"

"Yeah …"

"Well, wear glasses. Helps if you get pepper sprayed."

Queensway

The spy walks out into the sunlight, his beautiful surroundings doing nothing to inspire good behaviour.

A drive has taken over him recently, and it has something to do with Bex.

He wanders through Bond Street to Piccadilly and round the backstreets of Knightsbridge, taking what he likes – biscuit tins from Fortnum & Masons, books from the big Waterstones on Piccadilly, a silk scarf from Liberty's.

References to solar radiation control and weather warfare are written on a cashpoint in felt-tip pen. Anti-government tags have also appeared, scrawled over billboards and toilet doors.

A new block of luxury apartments opposite the Artemis shopping centre has been spray-painted with anti-Zionist sentiments.

Not much is left of the hollowed-out shopping precinct, save for a few chemists and an upmarket gift shop. Nationalistic themes predominate. Patriotism and fake nostalgia serving as a replacement for cultural identity.

He sifts through the overpriced tin openers and British flag-print cushions, waiting for the pub to open.

In the back corner of one of the tourist shops there's an array of hats.

He is magnetically drawn to the dome shape and slightly upturned brim of an imitation Lock & Co bowler, similar to the one worn by his recently vanished comrade. It's not a style he'd be caught dead wearing, due to its cultural connotations with the city's financial district, an area he's been obediently rebelling against since 2011. But he picks up the item nonetheless and turns it round in his hand, before self-consciously placing it on his head. He looks at himself in the mirror and is immediately struck by the change that seems to take over his whole atmosphere. He is momentarily filled with a sense of pride. In that split second, the uniform of business aligns him to a social tribe he is not entirely at ease with, implying as it does the glamour of crime and the power of economic security. He decides that he likes the hat, contrasting as it does with what has become his usual attire of drab functionality: the army surplus gear, dirty trainers and hoodie that form an activist's uniform of non-conformity. Instead, he sees what a proper cad of the late nineteenth century would've looked like.

"Suits you," says a voice behind him. Mckenzie flinches at the word 'suits', fearing for a second that he is being compared to that dreadmost thing, a capitalist. To his surprise, he finds himself pushing a crumpled tenner into the shop assistant's hand.

He steps out onto the Bayswater Road. Nowadays, Queensway is a stomping ground for corporate coffee chains and NGO beggars.

He clocks the older guy with dyed red hair standing outside the bookies on the corner, recognising the mahogany tint of his thinning hairline – he'd seen him at Parliament Square. Must have followed him from Oxford Circus.

Someone has written the words, '*They Killed Diana*' on the panel of a bus shelter.

He sparks up a cigarette and presses the 'record' button on his iPhone camera, aiming it vaguely in the stalker's direction.

Paranoid schizophrenics were always leaving messages for each other in bus shelters and charity shops. Some resorted to stickering, but a strategically placed badge on an old school blazer would do.

There were other clues on licence plates and well-timed songs by The Police. Nothing was an accident, and nothing was a coincidence. But to think they hired special agents to follow you round town seemed a bit far-fetched. The amount of co-ordination that would take. And yet, who was that strange man standing on the other side of the street? When you were in this line of work, you weren't paranoid, they really were out to get you.

It was a lilac-blue evening and the body was gone, the time was gone, the rebellion was gone.

At four o'clock he'd wanted to rewrite history, it had been such a long walk. His figure passing through Westminster Bridge like a ghost. The phone hadn't rung in ages, days, weeks.

He thinks he sees her in the doorway to a shop entrance, lighting up a cigarette, the face gone old and ancient, gorgon-like. Faces resembled each other. Was this imposter syndrome? The onset of dementia? Or his subconscious mind telling him he was going round in circles again?

Surely no one has ever willingly spent this many hours alone in a row. He walks down Camden High Street, past the recently painted rock club on the left, a few doors along from the Open University.

It had been too easy to leave without paying. The cinnamon bun and coffee had been free. Surely they meant for him to have it, or they wouldn't have made it so easy to steal.

Sitting there, he sips a cup of ginseng tea pondering on this new experiment with morality. On the balcony at that time of evening you can see out past the Holly Rood estate and onto the turrets of Greater London. He'll meet her again, a new way to break the stalemate.

A flat above the Electric Ballroom. Mongrel dogs – part Jack Russell, part crow.

That chick from the big demo. The one with the limp who'd been out with a murderer.

Why don't you get a cab to the hospital? Everybody loves to get cabs. Just behave like you're rich and you will be. That's how it works.

No, it doesn't.

It's ten past four and the phone hasn't rung in years, weeks. It hasn't rung in decades. Go out and buy some cigarettes.

I'm moving to the Caribbean, he decides. Nothing ever changes if you keep ringing the same people. Go back in time to that place. Did she call The People? The MOD?

That's an in-joke, because her name's really Dom, speaks in code.

"I don't give names to the EDL …"

I only wanted to see you, to spend time in your hazelnut mind. Your green shimmering skag-eyes. Your holographic head, your skunk psychosis. Let's do a whip-round.

Have you made it out yet? No, don't call me. Don't write back. I don't think I can bear to hear that you're doing well. May you be a hippie wreck living at your mother's forever.

It's not like I've moved on in life, although I do have a back-scratcher.

Maybe it's protection that she never contacts you …

On that cold day, she'd walked out into the bright sunlight of Holborn Circus.

"Nobody likes a grass."

The location of the stickers always indicated a certain attitude. A few years ago, when the signs came up round

London, maps of the area, certain messages had started appearing suggesting some anti-capitalist agenda, but then they had turned out to be a hashtag for a gastropub chain.

The new leader of the Seize Party is on the front cover of the morning paper, looking like an indie scarecrow. Something manipulative in the way he's being so often condemned. Feels like fake opposition. Paranoia? Or just discernment. Mckenzie can't quite tell.

He takes a closer look at the poster. #FINDBEX. It isn't her. Or if it is, it's an old picture, a Photoshop effort. He keeps it for argument's sake.

It reads as follows:

MISSING CAN YOU HELP?
This is Bex – last seen Sat. 3rd November at about 16.30 hrs.
Bristol Temple Meads.
- 28 years old- Wearing long dark coat and army-style boots
- 5'8" slim build
- Shoulder-length blond hair usually wearing a bowler hat
- Lip ring, cheek and nose piercing

With his pulse racing, Mckenzie goes to check her social media. Her latest tweet.

"This is Jarod. Bex's friend. Last night her car was found near Clifton Suspension Bridge. Memorial tomorrow at Parliament Square."

This time she's gone too far. Typical grab for attention. Bex is a liar, a trickster, after all.

He scrolls back a few posts, looking for some of her writing. The last post by her is dated 1st October. Impossible.

She'd been such a compulsive poster, social media being more like a diary for her in many ways. She never left it more than a few hours without writing something. In light of this new information, her Facebook feed reads more like a suicide letter.

His heart is now beating out of his chest. He decides to check Jarod's page. Sianne too. Both their profile pics have been changed to the Missing Can You Help poster.

A way to mark their respect, perhaps. He eventually finds the write-up by Himesh Vianney. Elegant, honourable. A tribute so beautifully worded, he decides it must be a joke.

Reverse

As he slowly opens his eyes, Compost Mckenzie becomes aware of the room around him. Purple and red like a womb. He fixes his gaze on the wall before him, where blue and gold painted symbols form an alphabet he's never seen before, but somehow intimately recognises. The cyphers pull him in, and he starts to feel extremely energised, as though he's drinking in knowledge through his eyes.

Something is different here. It takes him a moment. No more can he feel the ache behind his eyes – the itchy soreness, that sensation of having not slept. Then he realises what's missing. It is the sense of tiredness that he has been carrying with him for so long.

The dream had been psychoactive; treehouses and telepathy, hay bales, walkie-talkies. It's some sort of version of paradise. Surrounded by English villages and sunny fields. And then he remembers where he is, and that it hasn't been a dream at all.

"It's all about TEA," says the familiar girl with ebony-black hair and red lipstick. It's later that morning in the broken-down kitchen. That pinkish-brown background again. Paint peeling off the ceiling. She refers to habits and rituals, traditional needs, inherited patterns and failed coping mechanisms. A singing sort of voice, high-pitched like a child's.

"Our aim is consciousness-alteration. I used to drink black coffee until I hallucinated."

He has only just realised that she is topless. What surprises him is that he isn't in the least bit fazed by it, the Kundalini energy seems to have become evenly dispersed and balanced throughout his body. He sees things as though from above, with no anger or desire.

"Technically we're on a hill fort, so that's an advantage. The enemy will be exhausted by the time they reach the top. As for the land itself, it's a burial mound for Celtic kings and queens. A hermetic esotericist once owned the place and used it to perform his magickal operations. We found the castle during the first series of raids on major cities."

The year is not known, they tell him, though it's estimated to be somewhere around 2030. They do not have a plan, only an ancient stereo. For many months they have been journeying to find a cassette tape, rumoured to be a recording of The Queen. The last known transmission before the towers came down and the internet became obsolete.

As the girl continues talking, Mckenzie feels sure he knows her but can't say from where. It's as though she's a version of someone on another timeline – and then it hits him. She reminds him of his old friend Sianne Athers, but different somehow, in a different incarnation.

"Our ambition is to reverse all traditions and traits that keep us confined to destructive behaviours. We are an art collective, a sort of spiritual rehab, where self-induced curses can be reversed and healed, and along with them, the spell on London."

"London ..." says Mckenzie, who's still piecing things together from the night before, and thinks he must have had more to drink than usual.

"That's where I was. How did I ... I feel ten years younger," he says, and notices the sound of his voice isn't scratchy and hoarse like before. It sounds higher and lighter – as though he's never smoked a cigarette in his life.

It's a joke, clearly. They're some sort of experimental theatre company. A nudist art collective. Either that or there must have been something in the cup of tea she gave me, he reasons.

"London, you don't want to go there. It's been derelict for years, became a war zone after they evacuated all the refugees. The free people – travellers, like us."

"What happened?" he says seriously.

"Well, the war, of course. I take it you're a walk-in."

He looks at her but doesn't say anything.

"Though many didn't know it was a war at first," she continues. "After the rise of the Death Towers, they kept using their tags as usual. Many didn't pay heed to the warnings: the headaches, the seizures, the brain-fog. Nasty little things – everyone used to have them, they were better than a microchip because you didn't even need an injection. People just bought into them of their own free will."

"Then a load of people got sick and died," says a fair man with freckles and slightly sunburnt skin. He carefully fills the kettle with water from a hipflask.

"They didn't know they were turning themselves into mini antennae. And the ones that didn't get totally fried, well, they ended up getting drafted in as army workers, slaves. Too dead in the head to think for themselves, but good for doing basic civil service-type work."

"You're talking about mobile phones, the 'smart' phones."

"The spy-phones, yes. Tags," says the girl. "We only survived because we stopped using them years ago. And we have met before, you're right. I'm a shaman."

It's impossible that she heard my thought, thinks Mckenzie.

"No, not impossible here. We're more telepathic since those darker years. The radiation blocked our chakras, but we were always on our way to awakening. That's why they invented them, to keep us controlled; a prisoner to our 'cell'. We like to challenge all systems of control here."

"Welcome to COS. We are the Children of the Sun, a commune for the New Earth," says the sunburned man. "My name is Artemis."

"And I'm Kalitisi." As she says her name, Mckenzie gets several recurring snapshots of having known this woman in personal life; they've been friends for thousands of years, he's sure of it. He sees them living on a houseboat together in Bath, riding along the Nile, feeding kittens buffalo milk in India, drinking wine in Spain, where they have a farm, and five golden retrievers …

"We explore sexual taboos and practise yoga and fasting, we use shamanic trance dance to get into altered states," she says.

Mckenzie is starting to feel very queasy now. He leans against the wall for support, and as he does so, glimpses down at his body. He's wearing white silk lounging trousers.

"What about the police. Can't they use tracking devices to find us out here?"

"They're not even on our frequency," laughs the shaman. "You have nothing to fear. All we do here is meditate and love each other. We don't have locks on our doors, we don't have secrets, we've never been taught shame."

This sounds like actual hell, thinks Mckenzie. I must be losing my mind. But at the same time, he can't help but feel taken in by these beautiful people, they seem so kind and helpful; there's a magnetism to them that draws him in. And in that moment, he decides to forget that it bothers him and go with the lucid dream.

Before the tall gilt mirror, he sees himself. The lines on his face are less prominent, the skin more plump and taught where creases once were. No frown-lines where his eyebrows meet.

He steps out into the empty yard.

Alone at last. Suddenly it occurs to him. He reaches down into the deep pocket of his robe and feels the rectangular outline of a cassette tape. He's been wanting to listen to it for ages. And at last, he has found a stereo. When he plays it, he's amazed to hear his own voice played back to him. But a more aware, awake version of himself.

There are many other Children living at the castle. They sit around eating fruit and tell him of their philosophies. He is most intrigued by the mention of their leader, the founder of the thirteen temples of COS, Queen Hermes.

"You'll be amazed when you meet her, she's really friendly."

Mckenzie immediately sees an image of a statuesque woman, her face painted gold with purple eyes and metal plates on her teeth. A transgender warrior, a hypnotist healer.

"She's helped many who escaped the cities. She took down the towers with her servitors."

The multiverse, thinks Mckenzie. Temple cloud jester with a forked tongue. The thirteen dragons. Of course! Thirteen timelines, beginning at the Bishopsgate boundary, where she first laid her offering to the Serpent Gods.

"There is a difference between lore and statue," says a voice.

"Don't you mean Law and Statute?"

It means what you think it means.

"After her disappearance, some said she was still alive. Relocated and living under a new identity. We set up our own centre for behavioural change. She called us her tribe, the Children of the Sun. The dragons took down the Towers. It caused total chaos."

Somewhere in his mind, he dips into a memory. Sees tables, trays. A girl in a bowler hat. Could it be that this Queen and he had been associates for a time – contemporaries, even?

NASA

Bex lies on her side, smoking. The tiredness has at least stopped the visions. She's been wondering if it's possible her thoughts are being projected from microwave NASA technology in space.

The giant rig outside the window had gone up several weeks ago as part of the new Parkway shard. In the back of her mind, she suspects it's been fitted with a camera for spying, and then wonders blankly if they'd really go to all that effort.

NASA's a psyop. It's all a goddamn psyop …

Suddenly she lurches forward and rushes to the kitchen to pour water on her cigarettes, though she knows full well that later she'll be drying them off on the radiator. To ensure this ritual doesn't occur, she pours washing-up liquid over them and then douses them with hot tea.

Recently she's been remote viewing over Compost Mckenzie. She can verify this by checking his posts on social media, which reveal his actions. They often seem eerily connected to her own. She touches her toe; he mentions stubbing his. She goes to the fridge to get milk; he posts something about the evils of dairy farming.

But what use was this form of psychic spying if it couldn't be monetised somehow?

She'd responded to an ad for business support officer at MI5, but no one had replied. In the back of her mind, she knows she has an outstanding ability, and that if someone would only just believe in her, she could be of great service in this world, solving crimes and catching murderers.

The OCD goes reflexively to the most disturbing thought the mind can conjure. Like a nervous tic in the brain, returning to an image, the anxiety increasing in tandem with her attempts to shut it out.

The difficulty in being diagnosed with a mental disorder is that one starts to believe in the reactions of others. Of course, there is a side to Bex that believes she is not really doing secret intelligence work against the British government, and is in fact a paranoid schizophrenic sitting in a tower block. The doctors say that delusion can often be the result of trauma. Nowhere feels safe, so the afflicted creates a fantasy world because it's easier than dealing with life. But no one had factored in that she had the power to create her own reality and had now become what she claimed to be. The diagnosis had indeed been a curse, but it had also given her an identity, a harrowing tale she could use as a shield against her behaviour.

Over the years, her parents had listened with frustrated indifference as their daughter described the role she played as a spycatcher on the London protest circuit. The more successful she became among her peers, the more deluded she appeared to those on the outside.

Whenever she went home to visit, after a sectioning or for 'corporate rituals' such as Christmas, she was made to confront the existence of this parallel reality. Her life, to them, looked like living on benefits and eating from bins, the disappointment reflected in their faces increasing with each passing year.

The bedroom where she slept wasn't hers anymore; they'd put her up in the spare room. All her books and CDs were stashed in the attic. The red bedspread looked clean and uninviting. Not uncomfortable enough. She had transferred the blankets to the floor.

The Tricantamin certainly helped sedate her against the forced normality of it all. They didn't understand what she considered to be simple and plain. Trying to explain it was draining and often infuriating, it just made the psychosis worse. The fog that was over them had intensified at the same rate that the one surrounding her had dissipated. Bex didn't need more pills; what she needed was an exorcism.

Back in Hackney, the high street is its usual self. Psychedelic scarves in windows and Turkish Hammam baths.

Umut 2000 Ocakbasi and Restaurant. Next to a new building development called Fairview Homes.

Must get to the graveyard, she thinks to herself. At least the sleeplessness had bashed her brain in like a beer.

A muttering man in a tatty bomber jacket dodders down Crossway reading a copy of the latest free paper. For a minute she thinks it might be King Arthur dressed as a tramp in drag.

The vision returns, making her clench her fists until her fingernails nearly cut into her flesh. She rolls her eyes to the back of her skull and opens her mouth to scream but there is no sound.

Where are the visions coming from? Are they hallucinations? Are they being sent from somewhere? How could they do that?

Projected conversation. Inserted thought. Microwave technology. Nothing to do with the vulture-headed god she'd glimpsed outside the British Museum ... Must remember not to steal talismans from gift shops ....

It's easier to navigate the city when there are forces dragging you to graveyards to collect dirt to put into bags, but best not to tell people these things.

The mask is slipping, the magical personality she uses to persuade her friends and misdirect their minds, encoding specific symbols through the use of badges, brooches and T-shirt slogans.

In her head she replays a recent conversation with Compost Mckenzie. They'd been drinking their cups of strong tea in the hospital, discussing secret plots and cover-ups, crop circles and the benefits of psychedelics. She'd said he was pretty clued-up for a left-wing feminist. The subject had then changed from Golden Dawn kabbalah to the Bavarian Illuminati.

Her overconfidence after a night's drinking has put her at risk. She reminds herself that she got sectioned last year for punching her brother in the face following an argument over climate change.

She nervously scans back over the tweets she has no memory of writing.

'I knew too much so they locked me up.'

'Nice room here … More like a studio flat.'

'Out there isn't real freedom. Not at this stage in the game.'

'Bribery isn't working and blackmail is not my style, but you have to play to win.'

'Under Section 3 they can detain and admit me for up to six months against my will. Once in hospital, I do not have the right to refuse medical treatment.'

'There's no point denying it, they are being sent. Some of them are government employees; some just demonically possessed method actors. I regard them as a gift.'

'Soon I will go to the graveyard and get my guides to give me a refill. Talking to ghosts always buoys me up.'

'I recall what the doctors advised. Disguising traumas only makes them worse – it's better to try and find ways to explore them, through arts, crafts and cooking …'

'END MI5.'

'I will miss you all.'

They're playing a Turkish cover of "Could It Be Magic" at one of the cheap cafés near Abney Park cemetery. Wyverns like to sleep near graveyard dirt and are said to protect the city's hidden treasure.

But what good is money if all it does is leave you alone in a restaurant on a weekday morning with no job and seemingly no purpose except to change the world one slice at a time?

Mckenzie makes his way there, scouring charity shops for clues.

You got good little knick-knacks in Hackney. Little offerings to the Goddess, things Spirit left you.

There was a digital violence round Homerton. Trying to be something it wasn't.

"Dare I go to St Pauls?" he wonders. "No point, no point …" Something had jumped into him there, the eyes had started to take on the look of someone haunted.

It isn't until he reaches the post office that he realises he is talking to himself. He's forgotten to notice that his thoughts are coming out of his lungs through his mouth, and only cottons on because a few people have started staring. Observing the expressions of others is a way of discerning what is real and what is not. Did it matter, though? A social chain in his mind is holding fast to saying that it does. And is unbreakably sure that it does. Or, what if someone he knows sees him? Then it will be a case of Chinese whispers.

A part of him wants to care, but an even bigger part has become enlivened by how liberating it feels not to.

"I am 'one of those people'," he decides. "One who has let go of the very last aspect of social embarrassment, the need to be seen as acceptable."

The first thing he always does when he walks into a charity shop is to take a look at the DVDs.

Unless there's someone else there, which on that day, there is.

Usually, he'll go over and look at the clothes and books until the person has gone. But for some reason, on that day, he just wants to barge past and not wait and be patient.

He finds three titles that are things he's been looking for for ages. It strikes him as instantly suspicious that *Cradle of Fear*, *The Devils* and *Hidden Agenda* should all be in that one location, and the first thought that goes through Mckenzie's head is that someone has put them there intentionally to intimidate him. The same 'someone' who knows he's in cahoots with Bex Riley. They know about things like search engine preferences because they have all the devices monitored and apps with built-in surveillance – so it is completely reasonable for him to conclude this.

There are two things you can do in this situation. Go mad and tell the doctors. Or accept. You can choose to see it as damn good of them to do you a favour like this, by bringing something to your doorstep. You know you can't get out. They will always be there, and they want you to know they will always be there.

The dome of the mosque is visible above the rooftops of Shackelwell Lane. And he thinks that he too is 'shackled well', this time to the prison of obsession.

A number 236 pulls up and nearly clips a cyclist on the corner. He heads up Stoke Newington Road, writing the first part of a confession in his head, which he plans to burn and throw into the Thames as an offering to the Goddess Hathor. Truth be told, he's now more addicted to the sense of self-loathing that this act of destruction will bring.

A few streets away, Bex walks passed the downmarket beauty clinic that does THREADING, DERMTOLIGICA, HOT WAX and SHELLAC. A flustered woman with badly bleached hair runs out and picks up the placard for Christmas offers that has fallen down in the wind.

Locals wander the quiet market stalls; the young, upwardly mobile professionals have gone home for their holidays.

It all started with a basement conversion.

"What's that noise?" her keyworker had asked.

"Oh, they're building a house outside my window."

The noise had been going on in the background for so long it was beginning to make her go mildly insane.

Money was safer in bricks and mortar than it was in banks and offshore tax havens. Rooftop gardens and outdoor lighting, walls with in-built speaker systems. They were building a lift for the Bentley.

The interfering woman in flat 8 who'd found out that what they were doing wasn't exactly legal, but when she had tried to explain, they just bought the lawyers.

The chaos they were causing to the surrounding neighbours meant nothing. All that digging in the garden and installing cement had caused the rain to flood the surrounding area and led to subsidence. Cracks appearing in the walls, dust everywhere; even the lights had stopped functioning because of the vibration of the drills.

And all to protect the feudal corporate gated community within this new federal monarchy. Soon there would be a perimeter going around the city, and only the servants would live there.

She scans a news headline, staring past the screen, subconsciously aware of the imagery. Military-style police surrounding a well-known statue on Regent Street. The column of red text underneath issues an array of devastating headlines.

Certain people with mental problems can't not speak about it.

She's cold and alone and the soup hasn't warmed her. It's only reminded her body how tired it is.

"Go to the graveyard," says the wyvern. "There are thirteen dragons surrounding the Corporation of London."

Most of the exceptional minds are relegated to joblessness, and a larger portion of these end up on the streets, homeless in the freezing winter. Unable to return to their families for reasons she can well understand.

"It's all part of the global depopulation agenda," she tells him, but the man isn't really listening. He takes the card out of the machine and their fingertips smudge together in a way that feels too intimate. Awkwardly, she changes the direction of the conversation and tries to block out the voice in her head that says YOU WERE MADE FOR ME.

Compost Mckenzie. It's easy to imagine him being a plainclothes. But why here? Recently, she cannot be in a social situation without thinking people are secretly recording her.

Without

Black cars slide by outside a revolving door at the gallery on Euston Road.

It's the week before Christmas, and families have come to enjoy their holidays in this industrial Soviet-style setting. Wide white walls and an exhibition on asylums in a bleached white cafeteria. Luminous underfloor lighting and a pro-vaccination campaign disguised as an art installation.

Tall women with short hair come here to browse unusual items in gift shops and seek inspiration for their art fairs. The coffee is often not quite hot enough, which the staff say is for health and safety reasons.

Before they lived in the world consciously, there was a fault in the operating system. Now they'd been knocked off-centre; reactions were disproportionate and stronger, a condensed attunement. Outrage towards petty things, and not enough anger towards what really mattered. Exacerbated areas got misappropriated. It was like a reflex action that produced a trait they hadn't decided to monitor, or that they were unaware of.

He looks through the rental ads at the back of the paper.

Professional couple. Dead pool of stagnant slime. No light could reach it. Trapped air, dank gas, DVDs rotting into the body. Externally nothing could be detected, though through language there were scripts and mannerisms that betrayed a seeping bloodlust.

Watching things, listening to music, and then there's this look that passes between them, like they both know something. It's as though he and Bex have seen each other before, just several lives along. The thought alludes to something not easily worded. Words made it difficult; words made it less …

These were the moments missed, the indecipherable subtleties where there seemed to occur a crossing over of meaning as they peered between worlds.

He ponders the concept of the doppelganger. And later looks at the drawing tacked onto his wall. As he stares into the dark lines of scribble, he can make out different shapes appearing within it – an axe, a keyhole, the symbol for Pi.

He goes to the wall in the bathroom to take a look at the other drawing. But this one has a different atmosphere. Something about those concentrated layers of biro etched over and over to depict what might be the Georgia guide-stones.

Everything is owned, it's all monitored. Out there in the public domain, there's no privacy, and yet bizarrely, the citizens and even most of his friends are unaware or do not feel in any way alarmed by this encroaching utopia that's being forced upon them.

They grow accustomed to their state of self-imposed censorship. Those who are sensitive have to ensure a robust psychic firewall.

They are just coincidences, he tells himself. And yet he knows they are growing more frequent for a reason.

The intelligence services had no cause to infiltrate the very movements they set up. Most activists fell for it hook, line and sinker. He doesn't think of himself as a shill; he's a disrupter. One of Albion's army.

Trained professionals take over whatever grassroots cause it might be that's attempting to establish itself. They shut down any voice that questions the agenda of their drawn-out meetings. People liked to defer because deep down it is so engrained in the psyche from years of ritual conditioning, this sense of being led.

Again, he looks at the picture on the wall. Sellotape was so depressing. He must get to a point in life where he has a frame, not Blu-tacked scraps of Bex's old drawings.

It is someone's job to encourage a harmonisation between rival anarchist groups, but it isn't working out that way. Mckenzie's gone rogue.

They've wiped his record, and there's a payment, monthly, going into his bank account. Not a lot, but enough to know he's still working for them, whoever 'they' are.

Without an imagination, the city makes decisions for you. Streets and signposts positioned to help guide you towards approved destinations.

Wouldn't want you wondering off or traversing things in an unusual way; it might dismantle a pattern of thinking, and that can happen after you've been here too long.

There is another London which exists parallel to this one. Hidden and hinted at, it urges you to take more pagan paths and veer off in the wrong direction, trusting your feet as they trace underground rivers towards holy wells and memory tracks, until you reach a surmounted powerbase which overlooks the financial district.

On a nightly basis, Bex veers dangerously close to OD'ing on a cocktail of medication and alcohol, risking accidental death rather than outright suicide. She knows the consequence of the latter is to remain trapped in the fog of eternal return, and yet she must rid herself of something.

It is when in these altered states that she begins to feel aware of a presence. Something of serpentine form, bright grey scales and a set of curved wings. In the sparkling oil-slick eyes, she now recognises one of the guardians. They're not just statues.

Benevolent dragons looked after the gold of the city, that which made the culture rich. They protected the bohemians, the fragile, the weird, the lost.

After the botched eye test, she had begun to perceive things differently. At first it was clairaudient. The creature communicated its arrival through the sound of its breath: deep sighs like the ocean, long and relaxed. This was accompanied by the smell of the pink soap used to mop the floor in schools.

Then came the sense of immensity, its great wings hugging the sky. Creating bellows with its breath, enough to cause storms which took out churches and ripped down towers. Not always visible to the human eye, perhaps sentiently aware of its own fearsome appearance, it could alter consciousness, allowing itself to become invisible.

She writes all this down in her diary, sometimes returning to it later, having no memory of the encounter at all.

Upon awakening, she plans a prison break from her life. But she doesn't just want to keep moving from prison to prison, her life allocated by free travel and parking zones. Sometimes she can't see with this new vision and falls back behind the invisible bars, into the comfy swamp of addiction and routine. She forgets to take chances and go off-course again.

Trying to change the world has its upsides, but what was she drilling down to in herself? Although the old fight had proven illusory, the eye test has shone a light on her denial.

Her social media timeline reads like a suicide note. And it is indeed a death wish, a premonition. She knows the power of manifestation and yet does not pay heed to the warnings.

The outside prison was getting tougher, at the same rate as the one inside her receded. The dragon, the eye test, Compost

Mckenzie. Maybe it was all linked. To dissolve the bars of the prison within, one must first turn to the issue of control. Her obsession was keeping her captive.

The shaman drinks spirits, and psychiatric curses ensue. The afflicted inhabits two worlds: one in keeping with the overground reality, and another in which all paradox is possible.

This book is printed on paper from sustainable sources managed under the Forest Stewardship Council (FSC) scheme.

It has been printed in the UK to reduce transportation miles and their impact upon the environment.

For every new title that Troubador publishes, we plant a tree to offset CO_2, partnering with the More Trees scheme.

For more about how Troubador offsets its environmental impact, see www.troubador.co.uk/sustainability-and-community